THE ELECTRIC DWARF

TIM VINE

CROMER

PUBLISHED BY SALT PUBLISHING 2019

2 4 6 8 10 9 7 5 3 1

First published in Great Britain in 2019 by
Salt Publishing Ltd
12 Norwich Road, Cromer NR27 0AX United Kingdom

www.saltpublishing.com

Salt Publishing Limited Reg. No. 5293401

A CIP catalogue record for this book is available from the British Library

ISBN 978 1 78463 172 7 (Paperback edition)
ISBN 978 1 78463 173 4 (Electronic edition)

Typeset in Neacademia by Salt Publishing

Printed and bound in Great Britain by Clays Ltd, Elcograf S.p.A

To Mary Whitehouse CBE

'One of the great things about books is sometimes there are some fantastic pictures.'

GEORGE W. BUSH

THE ELECTRIC DWARF

A MODERN TALE FEATURING A SMALL RED HERRING

The man was panting as he scrambled up the bank towards the bridge, startling an innocent blackbird with a broken wing that sat in a bush. Dazed, he powered over rocks and shrubs, negotiating thick patches of inhospitable brambles before clambering awkwardly over an unforgiving barbed-wire fence. Glancing down at his hands and legs, he became aware of blood patches staining him, turning his trousers a warm wet camouflage. As well as a weird numb sensation there was a pervasive ache throughout his body, yet he couldn't perceive whether it brought him pain or pleasure. Any feeling he was experiencing flatly refused to transmit to, or accurately compute in his brain. A pronounced dullness deafened his eardrums, all senses suspended as if he'd been heavily anaesthetised, mummified in glue. This was a person in a state of shock, face pale as chalk, feeling detached yet acutely aware at the same time, trance-like. His hair was plastered onto sweaty forehead, dirt marking his left cheek above an unruly beard. A barren escarpment ahead of him led up sharply to a road, but before tackling it he stole a glance back at the scene on the rail track. Mangled train carriages were strewn across the lines in a zigzag, some slewed over each other like discarded Lego bricks in a child's playroom. Shards of glass peppered the ground, and a number of windows were hanging precariously from their frames, smashed and fragmented yet somehow still holding together like shimmering, jewelled jigsaw-puzzle pieces. As he looked down to survey the horrific carnage, the man saw – but did not register – various limp human bodies scattered about, nor did he hear the rising groans coming from the injured, which blended curiously to form a macabre choir of agony. Dense white smoke was emanating from somewhere in the epicentre of the crash, acrid and harsh in the otherwise pure country air, and an uneasy stunned hush enveloped the atmosphere as if a damp blanket had cloaked the surrounding locality. The spectacular wreckage of the train – dramatically derailed and concertinaed – appeared to be almost in miniature, so surreal and implausible, an extravagant scene from a movie set. The man paused as an uncontrollable tick forced his left eye to jerk with ludicrous and violent spasms, and he nodded his head in slow motion, taking it all in carefully, suddenly very aware of the fact that this was all his doing. This was the outcome of *his* actions, *his* intentions, an act initiated and carried out by *him*. The Lone Wolf had struck, almost without understanding. You see, he was neither a moral nihilist nor a *bad* man, but just quite simply a fucked-up cookie, that's all. Shielded within an eerie stillness, nobody noticed him as he turned to climb up to the road before brushing himself down and walking away.

Norman couldn't sleep. Yet another drink and drugs binge – this one enjoyed over the last few days – continued mercilessly to take its toll on his poisoned, frail brain. Sick internal organs had also suffered another brutal battering, and now the grim chemical hangover stubbornly refused to die. As a juicy, fat and particularly noisy fly smashed itself repeatedly against the bedroom window, Norman lounged around uselessly, barely paying it any attention. He lunged just once with a pathetic gesture as if he was swatting it. 'Bloody thing! It's like a cross between badminton and cribbage trying to get these bastards!'

He had always had trouble sleeping, before, and indeed after his habit of smoking fields of pot. It had started in childhood, when his bedside lamp was obliged to burn throughout the night or else he would never fall into the arms of Morpheus. His teddy Roger, a relic from an innocent era, didn't even provide solace from this condition. Even when he was an acne-ridden teenager, a radio would sing or the TV crackle, otherwise insomnia ruled. This particular evening had been painfully dull for him as he'd stayed in at his grubby flat off Portobello Road, and unusually there had been no visitors to pass the time with, drinking or taking drugs in his squalid living room, as was so often the case. Down below on the street the market traders were packing up after selling their last Chinese-made *I ♥ London* hooded tops of the day to a gaggle of keen, plump Spanish girls. The relentless London drizzle had at first been a fun novelty for them, but now they were cold and fed up. A tall Rasta with cigarette-ash grey locks shuffled nonchalantly past a couple of arty young men both sporting silly over-sized plastic glasses, angular haircuts and bright trousers that looked a couple of inches too short, as a noisy group of Moroccan kids on bikes that were too small for them raced by on their way back to the nearby estate. A young skinny dude with tattoos and a cravat darted off the pavement into the gutter to avoid the bikes, then lit a Camel Light as he crossed the quiet road, enjoying the first lung-full of smoke. In the distance an aggressive-looking Polish man sporting a *Taxi Driver*-style Mohican approached, an achingly beautiful yet cheaply dressed and bored looking girl draped on his arm. A shrill electronic shriek from Norman's phone abruptly cut through the relative quiet of his living room. It was an unwelcome call from his father, who again lectured him on his indolence and lamentable lack of effort with life in general. Tony had grown increasingly impatient with him over the recent months, and it was hardly surprising. Norman was painfully aware that his multi-millionaire father was on the brink of cutting him out of his will, with the possible intention of leaving his fortune instead to an array of deserving and not-so-deserving charities around the country. Norman's life had descended into a squalid existence of near chaos in which he somehow scraped together some kind of living from low-level drug dealing, supplemented by occasionally putting on *a night* locally. This would generally mean booking a DJ to spin a few records in the latest trendy bar if he could organise it for the evening, then attempting to sell various illegal powders to the assembled crowd. The downward spiral of his own rapidly-increasing use was becoming clear to everyone but himself; he shrugged it off, putting the large use of drugs on his part down to 'the job'. Most drugs flew up his nose or ended up in his lungs in the form of smoke. LSD was one drug, however, that Norman only took about every four years as 'that's how long it takes me to forget how full-on and scary it is, before I decide it might be a good plan to give it another try.' If he were ever to attend a Narcotics Anonymous meeting – which he never would – he'd more than likely turn up high; likewise, he'd be the guy that would bowl in pissed-up at an Alcoholics Anonymous group.

In physical appearance the nebbish Norman had recently changed, and certainly not for the better. Grotesque yet compelling, he remained ludicrously, laughably short, having always been vertically challenged for as long as he could recall. He luckily wasn't, however, so short that if he was sitting down and stood up he would actually shrink in stature, which bizarrely is the case for an unfortunate few. Weight loss had affected him – the once superfluous blubber around his middle flank and under a squat stubbly chin had disappeared, leaving unsightly loose skin flapping around without a lot to hang onto. Pathetic spikes of wispy facial follicle growth only just made it through a vitamin-deficient pallid skin, neither quite managing to form what could be regarded as a beard nor a coiffed unshaven *look*. Any youthful tone and colour in his cheeks that he may have once possessed had gently but markedly surrendered to the regular battering of general abuse and a wayward city lifestyle pushed to excess. His grey pallor was not a flattering one, especially on such a young man. Formerly alert and lively, darting eyes now seemed deadened, markedly shrunken and set back, their place now alarmingly misunderstood in his photofit-style ovoid face, segments of which refused to match naturally as they had once during his youth. Unhealthy, strange, grey semi-circles had appeared under his eyes in recent months, mottled like a lunar landscape, ominous indicators of an underlying condition darkly and secretly developing deep within his body. Generous thick brown hair that could be witnessed in serious school photos of the younger man had now radically thinned out, exposing the intolerable crust that was an excuse for his diseased scalp, which only just allowed greasy lank strands to dare sprout almost apologetically, resembling some unearthly variety of deep seaweed, and often snowing sizeable flecks of dandruff onto his dark collar. Any charm and charisma that he may have formerly possessed had been gradually drained out of his character by the magnetic drugs that he so adored, essentially leaving behind an inherently far more uninteresting being hidden in an oblivion of smoke. Needless to say, he looked as though he urgently required at least a fortnight's holiday in sunnier climes. The nickname, The Electric Dwarf, had followed him since his schooldays, haunting and irritating him, but never ceasing to entertain others. The *Electric* part stemmed from his insanely-charged demeanour after snorting speed. The *Dwarf* part, well . . . A peculiar homunculus was the Electric Dwarf.

The shabby rented flat was dark, and clearly on the small side for two grown (or nearly grown, in the case of one of them) men to be sharing. Stinking plates and bowls cluttered the sideboard, the grimy once-white plastic bin overfilled as usual, mainly with half-crushed beer cans that had been carelessly tossed over. Neglected take-away pizza boxes gently festered in the corner, crumpled, with cigarette butts loose inside, a science experiment in place. Norman's flatmate was out on a date, the first in two years. In his employment as a motorbike courier, Yatter had been one of the best, but ever since being knocked off his bike one crisp March morning near Hyde Park, he had suffered increasingly nasty flashbacks and panic attacks, and rarely accepted work these days. Before this he had always been lucky out on the mean streets, his only other collision being a bizarre minor incident with a milk float around 5 a.m. one morning, which subsequently caused more mirth than distress. Nowadays a heavy cloud of ongoing depression enveloped him, the general stress of his own existence outwardly apparent having permanently etched itself into his face, boring deep furrows and lines of worry. Yatter's only solace was his poetry-writing.

THE MOTORBIKE VIBES

How the beast rumbles beneath my groin!
Gas tank shines, flash, as a new coin
Engine screams, vibes feeling good
I love my bike, she knew that I would.

I love my bike, I knew that I would
She smells, I sniff, she says that I should
Shift into gear, all vibes are good
I love my bike, we knew that I would.

by Yatter

His continuing use of drugs as a prop for his misery might fulfil him momentarily and provide ongoing occasional relief, but it was also taking its toll on his delicate psychological state, as well as his general physical health. The two of them had their rows, but generally got on, largely due to their mutual enjoyment in partaking of the same drugs. Norman and Yatter painted a funny picture when out together. Yatter would tower over everyone, whilst people generally ignored Norman, often barely noticing him, unless to nudge a friend and share a chuckle at his appearance. This had got Norman's back up more than once, to such an extent that he now rarely invited Yatter along if he was going out somewhere.

Norman couldn't sleep. He deftly rolled a joint and reached for the TV remote. There was a documentary about a triple murder, with a Philip Glass-esque soundtrack, intended to give it gravitas. Everything appeared to have become so *safe* on TV; even Art had conformed to the maximum in this risk-averse culture. Still, murderers were 'up there' with the list of other public hate figures, which now encompassed politicians, bankers, paedos, landlords, terrorists, hipsters and, to some . . . immigrants (or were they refugees?). Norman felt uncomfortable and switched over. Flitting between a John Lennon retrospective and *Peter Andre: the Next Chapter*, he sparked up and relaxed. John and Peter both started to irritate him in their very different ways. He ventured up a channel to see Freddie Mercury, who practically exploded out of the screen larger than life as if in 3D, on stage at a mid-80s gig from Rio. Norman turned it up. Although not particularly a massive Queen fan, he was transfixed by the undeniable charisma of the sweating singing star and his solid band of hair, and found himself deciding to pick up a copy of their *Greatest Hits* sometime soon, preferably on vinyl. Why were there no bands around like that anymore, with that amount of raw talent? A little while and another joint later, it seemed more likely to him that perhaps sleep could now be achieved, so without washing or brushing his nicotine-stained teeth, the stoned little man floated effortlessly into his bedroom and climbed into bed, removing a porn DVD *Chew the Fat* from his pillow, soon to drift off to a better place in a catatonic stupor. The dusty TV with its greasy, smeared screen blasted out *Death Wish* 4, unapologetically flooding the deserted room with violence.

Norman's father had had enough of his son's laziness. His habitual apathy clashed with Tony's work ethic and his attitude to life that he held dear; indeed, the very principles that had aided the ever-increasing rise in profits at the company that he'd set up many years before as a young man. Tony considered himself an altogether fair yet strict parent, any harsh words or hard discipline was only ever meted out for the overall benefit of his children. Besides, the distinct absence of affection shown by him to Norman would never cross his mind as being lacking in any regard, as it had been how his own father had been with him many years previously.

Tony was equally as stressed out regarding the current behaviour of his beloved daughter, who had regrettably hooked up with a rather strange character called Brian, a middle-aged bearded vegetarian who she had met on the Northern Line somewhere near Clapham. Perhaps if she hadn't had lost her balance and reeled backwards, flailing her arms as the train jerked sharply on that Special Day, she would never had tried his home-made hummus, his courgette fritters or wonderful tofu curry. Wearing sandals without socks, as he nearly always did, a direct hit scored by Polly's high heel had barbarically torn Brian's defenceless big toenail, ripping it clean off as she tumbled onto the filth of the tube carriage floor, down by his bloodied hairy foot. For a split second, as she clumsily pulled herself to her feet, Polly glanced at the unknown, unshaven man who she had inadvertently hurt and felt a strange jolt of joy – a pang of guilt-free pleasure. 'I never liked that particular nail anyway,' Brian calmly quipped as he winced, trying to ignore the sudden rush of intense pain. She grinned back involuntarily like a lovestruck teenager. The unusual encounter would lead to a surprising and intense sexual encounter only hours later at Brian's flat, such immediacy and liberalism highly unusual for both parties involved. Polly's insistence in helping him home made for an entertaining hobble through a maze of south London residential streets, with the princess propping up her prince who was dripping a trail of blood all the way to his front door. Then followed an almost ritualistic washing of his feet – delicate, sexy yet efficient on Polly's part – painful and highly erotic for Brian the recipient. Acted out by the pair of them, their actions had the distant abstraction of a dream, and it seemed to be the very cleansing act itself that was steadily and enjoyably guiding them both to its inevitable, beautiful and sybaritic conclusion.

The intoxicated pair were recently back from a religious camping retreat in Wales, and Polly had sent her dad a postcard that had disturbed him as it suggested that Brian the vegetarian might be *the one*. However, Brian painted for Tony the worst image of a son-in-law that he could ever imagine, and was without doubt nowhere near good enough for his little girl. The two men were off each others' radars in terms of world outlook, humour, sentiment and ideas, to such an extent that on the three brief occasions that they had met, disagreements were avoided only by the pacifying tact of Polly and her deft skill at swift subject-changing. This familiar conflict-avoidance tactic was something that she had been forced to hone throughout her childhood, often keeping the peace between younger brother Norman and their father. Now Brian seemed to be filling Norman's boots and taking on his role when they were with Tony, and she sensed that it would be only a matter of time before it kicked off between the two of them. For the time being, however, things appeared to be rolling along fairly smoothly, with both sides not rising to each other's bait. However, she had little idea about the important and life-altering ultimatum her father was planning to issue to her before the week was up. He was intending to take Polly and Norman out for dinner, and inform them that they were both to be cut off from his Estate, unless:--

Tony was to stipulate that the Electric Dwarf had to cease all his current drug-related activities, move out of London and find himself some genuine employment. For her part, Polly was now obliged to cut all ties with Brian, as well as promising to sever all future relations with the man - his sandals, beard and everything that accompanied him. They all agreed on an Italian place near Victoria Station that Tony had been frequenting for years, nearly always ordering the same dish - meatballs. He raved about them loudly at every visit to each bemused waiter, insisting on 'compliments to the chef.' He would never have a suspicion that they were inexpensive, frozen meatballs from a sprawling cash & carry in Wembley, put together with zero love at a nondescript meat-processing packaging plant on the edge of a grim industrial estate in Milton Keynes, bought in ugly plastic sacks for industrial freezing.

'The provenance of the meat?' I hear you ask.

Back to plate, confused waiter, microwave door shuts, heat! Aaaggghh, events are taking a terrible and unexpected turn. what's all that sauce? out into a fridge, nestling between huge butter slab and unidentified plastic storage container, out back into kitchen, it goes dark in a sack surrounded by other meat-balls, then a long wait, freezing cold! are we in a lorry or van? here we go, we are driving, out of vehicle, another inordinate wait, then I'm being pulled apart viciously in a series of machines, mixed up again and again, this is hell, what are all the powders that keep getting poured over me? in a bag, another drive, what the . . . ? blood, so much blood, agghhh, I'm pulled together, I'm a cow my God! walking backwards . . . all the others are so scared, waiting, I'm so hungry, beaten, back in a stinking lorry with no air, long journey it's horrible, stop, more driving, some grim holding area, water – at last, and a tiny bit of food, back to a filthy overcrowded shed, there are thousands of us, food, days turn to weeks, months, water, I am getting small, smaller, I fall, Mummy, is that you? I am sucked upwards into a wet and warm comforting place . . .

It was true, however, that the chef achieved results and was deft with the microwave, so perhaps should indeed be applauded. He had a great skill in knowing exactly the combination and number of minutes and seconds for anything that came his way. Some put it down just to experience, but he really was special. Plates were certainly never returned to the kitchen with a 'table four's complaining that their dinner's not hot enough, Chef' from a waiter. This was Norman's first square meal for some time, as he generally lived on sugary supermarket-branded yoghurt or white toast with margarine whenever he felt the urge to eat. Eating – or, rather, nutrition – for him was a slight aggravation bred out of necessity, intruding into his life rather than being a pleasure in it. But on this occasion, peculiarly, he enjoyed the meatballs in particular.

Over the just-defrosted tiramisu, Tony dropped the impending bombshell on his two stupefied offspring. Polly – who had felt that something was brewing, was fuming inside, but she bottled up all the anger as her faith and character insisted that she must. Such intense personal restraint wasn't always healthy and it certainly left her with many issues to deal with, when perhaps she should have had a good shout or wobbled through a self-purging row with somebody. Instead, a straining vein in her delicate and slender neck appeared to throb and bulge from nowhere, and she became aware of a sudden and unwelcome dampness under her armpits. Norman was too weak and emotionally crippled to complain, and besides, he felt that his father's wishes had been expressed with an indisputable air of finality, certainly not inviting any questions or debate. He was, for once, correct on that score. Tony had decided that he had put up with too much nonsense from his two beloved children, and recently he'd not been enjoying the realization that comes to us all that he wasn't going to be around on this Earth forever. Led by both his paternal instincts and a misguided intention of improving his children's lives, Tony had rashly decided upon this thinly-disguised attempt at blackmail.

With an ugly scrape of her chair, Polly got up, grabbed her jacket and shiny bag, turned on her heels and spat out an abrupt and near-sarcastic 'Thanks for dinner, Dad, I've gotta run. See ya, Norm, gimme a ding sometime.' Then she disappeared out into the night, still thin-lipped with scarcely-hidden fury.

The two men remained at the table and sat together uncomfortably. They could have been players in a Harold Pinter scene. It had been many years since they'd been together at a mealtime, and once the usual *conversation* would have consisted of Tony dishing out endless advice to Norman that was generally rejected before it had even been uttered.

'Best to just leave it now, Dad,' mumbled the son meekly, like a boy under half his age. 'I think I'll be off too.'

Less than an hour later, a louche Norman was giving a watered-down version of the evening's events to Yatter while chopping out their second line of speed. 'Maybe the old boy has got a valid point, I mean look at the state of me. I'm not exactly early twenties anymore, I shouldn't be doing this shit,' he rattled, as he wolfed up a huge line of off-white powder through a grimy ten-pound note. He offered the remaining slightly skinnier line to Yatter. 'Here, mate, get your laughing gear around that, son!' Norm stretched and watched Yatter lumber across to the table and greedily hoover up the offering.

'How about a trip somewhere to have a massive and final blowout, a two-week binge without restraint? I'll just take all the drugs I can find, and then some. Stay up two weeks solid, something like that. I might even get laid for a change, you never know. Then I could come back, move to Dulltown and find me a sensible nine to five, if anyone'll have me. Los Angeles always beckons and last time I tried to go . . . well, you know what happened. Bollocks, I'll probably go to Agricultural College for a year and become a farmer!'

'Mazel Tov, Norman! That's a great plan,' Yatter commented snidely.

'Mazel what? Sounds like a Cold War machine gun, you know, the famous killing machine, the Mazeltov BR38. Fully automatic 7.62mm cartridge, rarely jammed, short recoil, fairly lightweight for back in the day considering its firepower . . . '

'You knob!' was all Yatter could utter, chuckling as he brushed his nostrils and snorted vulgarly.

Norman's brain was processing and spewing out a torrent of information at breakneck speed, and Yatter turned his head away as Norman's words washed over him. This was, once again, a whirlwind of irritating and useless pondering that Yatter had to endure . . . but he had forced himself to put up with it and had built up a strange yet necessary tolerance as far as Norman was concerned.

A couple of years before, Tony had sponsored Norman a ticket to LA for a summer school, but his idea monumentally back-fired. At the last minute, with plans made and bags packed, Norman had been forced to send his father a text. He preferred it this way rather than face his wrath over the phone. It read:

> *technical hitch . . . I'm not going to LA as student visa declined due to arrest a couple of years ago. Sorry*

Tony's immediate disappointment swiftly turned to anger, and Norman's subsequent avoidance of his calls and messages for the following few weeks only managed to fuel Tony's mounting fury.

Norman simply went on living from day to day, with nothing particular of note in his life, no remarkable events or points of interest, nothing. As the drugs fuelled him, the bumbling dwarf drifted through the months without really noticing time slipping away. It seems that many people's lives – or existences – pan out in such a manner. There isn't a suitable piece on a chess board that conveys and represents Norman's unimportance in life; even the lowly pawn quietly holds too much potential for a reasonable comparison. Even when living day to day in a great city such as London, his effect on any one of his ten million or so neighbours was negligible. The great masses in city apartments packed into their tiny boxes like bees in a honeycomb, swarm to and from work like contestants in some nightmare reality TV show, although this *is* their reality, their boredom. Should glimpsing a Z-list 'celebrity' filming a commercial outside the Argos in Aylesbury truly be the highlight of someone's year? Or witnessing a punch-up in the Morrisons car park in Dollis Hill, or perhaps a crash on the southbound M1 carriageway? Such inane, mundane lives, so many human beings . . . a species that ticks along with the supermarket tills beeping, the gas bill at the crematoriums always rising. Do the managers of these death tidiers fix their energy tariff for a few years in advance, and are they eligible for a preferential rate, as faithful and reliable customers?

Norman had actually applied for a job once in his life. He'd managed to get an interview with the Area Manager at the local DVD rental place a few years previously, when such places still existed. Now, this guy *must* have been bullied at school; he resembled the overly-styled nerd type that had recently started to crop up in the background of so many trendy TV commercials. He spoke in a monotone, sounding as if he needed to clear his throat, but never did. 'So Norman, tell me, how would you deal with someone who wanted to rent a DVD?' Norman was a bit taken aback by the question and couldn't quite tell if it was a trick or whether it was serious, as it appeared so inane. He decided to take it at Face Value. 'Well, I'd probably say 'Welcome to Acadia Entertainment, are you looking for something specific, sir?' Then I'd maybe suggest a title or help the customer find what he was looking for, throwing in a quick 'Good choice!' as he approaches the counter. I'd offer the usual extras – sweets, crisps, ice cream or a 2-litre bottle of Coke for him to wash the movie down with, and then accept payment when he was ready. Terms concerning the return of the DVD would briefly be explained and a cheery 'enjoy it, see you soon' might be offered at his departure. Something along those lines, I'd imagine.' Norman had a hard time going through the process without laughing, but was sure that this was what Mister *Blend-into-the-Crowd* Area Manager wanted to hear. He subsequently could never figure out why he wasn't hired for the position.

On another occasion, an old school friend roped Norman in to help paint his aunt's shop just off the Fulham Road. Norman thought that it might be a chance to do something a bit different, so he turned up on the Tuesday in his painting gear. Tight, disgusting brown jogging pants from Oxfam and a ludicrously large T-shirt brashly emblazoned with a Polish Judo Club's logo completed the ensemble. It seemed like a 'bit of a laugh' at the time, but it really was not a good idea to emblazon A-R-M-A-G-E-D-D-O-N on the wall in metre-high black letters before starting to paint. It was only several days and many coats of paint later that the outline of the letters was not somehow still stubbornly poking through, visible to all. Needless to say, that marked the end of his brief decorating career.

Recently, the most effort that he had made to become gainfully employed was six months or so ago. A late-night post on Facebook: *I guess I need to get a job. Fairly lazy and no ambitions. Any suggestions/offers?* Funnily enough, there were no takers.

The Dwarf's sadly lost potential was that he had once shown promise as an Artist. Not as a painter, but as a youthful stoned man whose thoughts sometimes drifted towards rather interesting ideas. For instance, when a lively sixteen-year-old at school, his class had been instructed to build a model of something for an art project. His industrious classmates put in the effort and spent hours drawing plans, painting, gluing and building various structures. They produced aeroplanes, bridges, an impressive helicopter and even a dinosaur. It may have been born out of laziness, but Norman's plan was brilliant. These were the step-by-step instructions to build his model:

Blow out an egg.
Colour it all around with an orange felt tip pen.
Lay it on a small bed of cotton wool.
Cut a piece of white card about the size of a business card.
Lay the card in front of the model, as if an exhibit label in a museum or gallery, with the words BAKED BEAN – SCALE 1:80.

Unfortunately, the Head of Art had not appreciated The Bean, and Norman had been sternly told off rather than praised and encouraged.

A half-hearted attempt at a German language course, a determined mission to get fit which lasted three days, the endless intention to learn the guitar, a yoghurt-producing business that never passed the pub-table planning stage one evening, that first and final painting evening class, a market stall on Portobello Road selling something as-yet-to-be-decided, a DJ management agency, the start-up company that would produce alarms to warn that the bath was overflowing, a car wash, Christmas tree importing, a druggie destination-holiday specialist travel agency, and a gourmet marmalade suppliers were just a few of the pie-in-the-sky projects that Norman toyed with but never furthered. He harboured wildly fantastic ideas that he would one day become some sort of enterprising Bill Gates character, and although the dream had been formulated, the reality was that he may as well imagine that he'd become the next Archbishop of Canterbury.

Even so, there was something about one particular profession that fascinated Norman. Whenever he took a trip to the dump, all the guys who worked there appeared unreasonably jolly, upbeat and satisfied with their work. Whether it was by helping an old lady unload garden waste into a skip, or heaving an unloved rusting refrigerator onto a squeaking trolley, these guys never had a bad *vibe* about them. Could it be the fact that they were generally outdoors, doing something physical, also sociable? The criteria added up to a fairly rewarding job if looked at objectively, and on the rare moment that he pondered attempting some genuine honest employment, these factors hadn't escaped Norm . . . but then he'd roll a spliff.

Norm still hadn't asked his flatmate how his date had gone, and this finally got Yatter's back up. 'So when are you gonna ask me about the date, Norm?' Norman looked ever so slightly taken aback. 'Oh sorry, mate, with all this family shit I forgot to ask.'

The truth was that the evening had been far from a success. The girl in question – Caroline – was a lot plainer than Yatter had remembered from the motorcycle courier's office where she worked as a secretary, and out and about she had a strangely dominant and matronly way about her that completely turned Yatter off, irritating him somewhat too. She was a big classical music fan, and had insisted on picking up tickets for an evening of Beethoven and Brahms at a church in North London. As the interval approached (and not soon enough), Yatter was glad to notice a few wine bottles, boxes and an array of glasses neatly set up in a side aisle. As polite ripples of applause were dying down, he grabbed Caroline to get to the bar before a queue formed. Over his rancid glass of red – which incidentally had been invaded by tiny pieces of cork that bobbed around like plastic toys in a baby's bath – and her orange juice, he took the rare moment to actually speak to her. 'Did you clock the jazz bassoon moment towards the end there?' Caroline studied him blankly. She hadn't noticed the sketchy efforts from the woodwinds in the final movement of the concerto. He tried a different tack. 'Have you seen how dusty Jesus is up there on the rood screen? I want to get a ladder, a bucket of hot soapy water, climb up there and give him a bloody good wash! Look at that dust on his chest!'

Caroline was not impressed. 'Ssshh, you can't speak like that,' she chastised him.

'Or I could start with his feet, and maybe sherry vinegar would be better?' The evening was becoming tedious. She was clearly boring and he felt like winding her up because she took herself far too seriously. More importantly, he had decided that he didn't fancy her with even one bone in his body. Soon the serious-faced musicians were filing calmly back to their places for the second half, sitting down and tuning their instruments. This ritual contained Yatter's favourite music of the concert – the short-lived but exciting din of the orchestra's pushing and twisting, blowing or scraping their precious jumbles of pipes and Heath Robinson contraptions somewhere approaching 'in tune.' What a pile of mushy, sentimental wallpaper paste followed! A Brahms violin concerto, with some flash South American soloist who Yatter imagined all the female members of the orchestra fancied, and no doubt some of the male ones too. He was not at all impressed by the man's never-ending scraping, particularly his dire tuning problems when double stopping, however technically brilliant. Pathetically, the orchestra didn't even have a sexy cellist to ogle when the music became interminable. This is a requirement that many believe every orchestra must provide, and Yatter was very disappointed as it's always the fallback entertainment. He found a chewed-up pencil in his jacket and contented himself with scrawling a poem about tea on the back of the programme, just to pass the time.

THE TEA SONG

Coffee doesn't float my boat
Just leaves deposit in my throat
When I'm down I go to town
And drink more glorious tea!

The hotness and the wetness are insane
Beats beverages just so lame
You can tell a Real Man
He loves his tea, just like me!

These drinks that just aren't meant to be
Make one wretch until down upon one knee
Or else it's simply pee and pee
O, Bring me Glorious Tea!

Fizzy, chilled and sweet don't work
Fabricated by some berk
T – E – A *I love you so*
O, bring me more Glorious Tea!

By Yatter

Immediately after the music finished, Yatter made a feeble excuse and unceremoniously left Caroline at a bus stop. He was really useless with the opposite sex, on many levels. His parting thoughts made her blood boil: 'The concert was crap too . . . we should've gone to Camden to listen to some bell-end who can't even tune his guitar sing about how nice he smells.'

She swore at him under her breath for the whole bus ride home. It was only two stops. Meanwhile, as a fire engine belted past, brash siren demonstrating the Doppler effect perfectly with its comical urgency, he jumped down into the nearby underground, enjoying the welcoming and familiar rush of warm air against his face. Sitting across from a perfectly cool young couple on the rattling train, he wondered how much more money the guy had paid for his new jeans to have strategically placed rips in them. Had he stumped up four or five times their real value for the sake of a few tears, and for the pleasure of being served by some freaky bird with an aggressive haircut and alien-like make-up in an achingly trendy Shoreditch boutique? Most likely. They also appeared to be dangerously tight around the crotch area. Isn't there going to be a small legion of infertile men in their 20s, all brought on by the fashion for tight or skinny jeans? He also couldn't figure out why they were speaking English to each other even though he was sure that they were both Japanese, or how they could really be having an animated discussion about egg timers. There was an Odd Couple standing, clinging to each other. Him . . . so bean-like and high. Her . . . rotund and red. Together, they made the number 10. London life is never dull. Before he realised it, he was back at the flat.

'Well Norm, it was pretty shit,' he reported. Norman hadn't asked him anything about the date because he'd forgotton about it. Yatter was irked.

'I've had worse,' encouraged Norman. 'At least you didn't

sit on her lap and then puke down her shiny ballgown. You also didn't tell her that the only way you'd fuck her would be if she found you an Ecstasy tab.'

'You bastard! You've done that?' Yatter asked, laughing.

'Afraid so, geez, but it's nothing I'm proud of. Years ago . . . funny shit looking back on it though.'

'I guess it wasn't so cool when I threw up in someone's handbag upstairs on the bed at a house party – well, the bathroom was locked! Shit, I even rode home that night, well pissed,' Yatter recalled, with a mild pang of guilt.

It was the drugs that were yet again annoying Yatter. It had now got to a stage that he craved peace and quiet, and no Norman. Since Norman never invited him out anymore, their friendship had cooled a little, even if they still managed to share a joke from time to time. Norman was now still trying to figure out his plans, talking about a foreign trip for a final drugs binge.

'D'you know, Norm, that's a great idea, go for it. Try Ibiza or Thailand or something. You'll have a right laugh, and bring back some warm weather, will you?'

'Yeah, maybe something like that. But, you know, the weather thing,' Norman paused for effect, 'I already checked that with UK Customs. Bloody red tape, they don't allow any weather imports or exports of any kind, and the law's not set to change anytime soon.'

Yatter smiled as Norman snorted on his giggles. Yatter was on a mission to quit all the poison, but with the Electric Dwarf as his flatmate, this wasn't likely to happen anytime soon. His encouragement was purely selfish and largely but unconsciously driven through self-preservation, and he was already hatching a plan to take over the flat on Norman's relocation to Dulltown. He was even starting to imagine who he might find as a new flatmate. So it was that night, fuelled by drugs, that Norman's immediate future plans were collectively hatched and planned out.

'JESUS, FUCK! Welcome to France!' The words blurted out involuntarily, and Tom's heart skipped a beat. 'Shit the bed! We haven't even got our health cover sorted and the natives are driving like fucking maniacs!' A battered and ageing Peugeot hurtled around the blind bend towards them whilst overtaking an equally battered and ageing van. Tom was quick to swerve, nearly tearing his slightly-too-tight jacket at the shoulder seam. A trip down a ditch was narrowly avoided, more by luck than judgment. A brief glimpse of the driver showed Tom that the bizarrely irate female driver was yabbering into her mobile phone and smoking a Gauloise as if it was 1984, but he wasn't also aware that she had enjoyed a sociable and boozy extended lunch. He would recognise her a few days later as the secretary at the local Mairie, and this near-miss taught Tom an early and invaluable lesson about countryside driving customs in the area. Late one morning many months later, Tom lay sprawled out with limbs hanging in all directions. With a belly full of red wine, sleep – or at least some kind of state of unconsciousness – came swiftly. He had recently been out of sorts and had enthusiastically taken to the bottle this particular evening, and not for the first time. He and his long-suffering wife were part of a large exodus of British people who had moved to the French countryside, tempted by repeated daytime-TV promises of a 'dream life in France'. The vast majority of these expats would never have even vaguely entertained the prospect of relocating to France had it not been for such cheap and tantalizing productions that never seemed to be off TV screens around the millennium. Puzzlingly, a large number of this stream of arrivals could not even string a sentence together in French, yet they wrongly assumed that this would not cause too much of a problem either for themselves or for the bemused and occasionally bitter locals. Sue had left a disappointed lover back in England, a builder named Phil who was still listed in her mobile phone contacts under David: work (just in case). Still, Sue and Tom were enjoying their new life, and Tom felt more able to launch into his ridiculous racist rants in the French countryside as he received less opposition than back at home in the UK. This was mainly because he was not understood due to the language barrier, a hurdle that intimidated and shamed him. Sometimes perhaps people were too polite to disagree, he thought, or maybe his audience felt the same way, so listened in tacit approval. Little did he know that one set of his neighbours would use a thinly-disguised racist expression when discussing the English family next door: 'Mieux un anglais qu'un arabe' ('We'd rather be living next to an Englishman rather than an Arab.') These were people who rarely ventured out of the commune, occasionally took a trip to a nearby town, but would not go further. They had never set foot in Paris, and certainly hadn't travelled abroad. The clear irony of the fact that he was an immigrant in France was lost on him, and – as he often reminded anyone who would listen – the once Great Britain had obviously 'gone to the dogs.' A number of the expats he met were actually not far away from sympathizing with his train of thought, even if they were maybe a little more restrained in their shouting about it, but he missed his football mates he used to go to the game with, and of course the pub before and after the match. The UK's problems were one of the primary reasons that they had deserted their own country in the first place. However Tom's outbursts on this matter were becoming increasingly frequent and aggressive, mainly regarding 'bloody immigrants', often causing his wife Sue dreadful embarrassment. It became the usual event whenever he'd been drinking, and that was nearly every day as soon as the sun had gone down. Cheap wine and a destructively crippling ennui were the catalyst, and he was knocking it back in large quantities as if it were beer. It appeared to have become his personal mission to make a noticeable dent in the European wine lake, and he'd certainly been putting in the hours to this end. The same could not be said, however, for his work hours. The once seemingly fool-proof plan of setting up a plumber's business locally had backfired colossally, with sky-high social charges plus additional French taxes combining and conspiring together against him, dealing out regular crippling blows and bringing him to his knees financially. French clients were scarce, mainly due to his lack of ability to communicate with them, and few of the English expats now ever seemed to have any money, or at least pretended not to have any. Unusually, Sue was feeling that she had become unnoticed by her husband - certainly unappreciated. 'And what's that smell?' Tom blurted out, nearly shouting.

'That, my dear, is the wonderful fresh air of the countryside,' replied Sue with a well-honed sarcasm, developed after years of marriage.

Tom had been spending increasingly longer stretches hanging out with his new English mate Keith. Keith was the village expat boozer, a man who - however drunk the night before - would be seen without fail back on his patch at the bar the next afternoon. Only speaking a bare minimum of French, he would astound and sometimes disgust the locals with his stamina, while living out his twilight years blatantly flying in the face of all medical advice. He was an absolute trooper who would never miss a good day's skinful of booze, chuffing enthusiastically on fat cigars whenever possible. Despite nudging sixty-five, Keith's attire was that of a much younger man. As a huge Ferrari fan, he would rarely be spotted without his trusty red baseball cap, and often wore ridiculously ill-fitting sportswear. Over at Tom and Sue's place, he'd often turn up and make himself more than welcome.

Tom and Keith had been on the sauce all afternoon this particular Tuesday. Tom sauntered back from the kitchen with another couple of ice-cold tinnies.

'Job's a goodun. Bring it on, Keith!' They cracked open the beers.

'I think you'll find I'd make a bloody great football hooligan, me,' claimed Keith with his lairy manner, sporting the red Ferrari hat. 'I mean, at the end of the day, all things considered, the main problem is that I'm just not into the bloody football part of it! I mean, just between you and me, right? You just go up North, or to some other no-good team in London, just for a fight. D'you even actually bother with the football bit?'

'Oh you twat! Of course, but I guess you wouldn't understand, you old git,' retorted Tom, slurring a little. 'Stick to your racing cars.'

'And this football shite. Look at it, come on. Let's look at it, you know . . . objectively. How the hell can you actually choose a team to support? Nobody seems to root for their local team, it's not like the centre forward might be your neighbour or anything . . . I mean all it is, it's money . . . business . . . *bullshit.* Whichever bloody team's got the most dollars buys the best players. Put a load of best players on one team . . . make more money. *Bullshit.* Why does someone living in Cornwall support Manchester United, for fuck's sake? Someone in Liverpool support Chelsea? I'm not one to make a mountain out of a molehill, but even looking at it through rose-tinted specs are you sure it's nothing to do with the small fact that they might win, perhaps?'

Keith was enjoying becoming ever more arch and sarcastic, riling Tom.

'You wouldn't understand,' Tom replied weakly. 'It's . . . well, it's about the players, and the style of the team. And, well . . .' He had a habit of not finishing his sentences.

'Naaa, I mean, at the end of the day, I think you'll probably find that that's all a load of . . .' he paused for effect, '*bullshit.*' Keith assumed a Dalek-like voice for this final word.

'Or you might follow the team your dad supported or something like that . . .' Tom tried to think of a good reason to revoke Keith's attack, but was finding it hard. 'Still, you're just being miserable. It's like wading through treacle talking to you. A bloody pessimist, that's all you are. It's actually fun, the game, believe it or not, maybe that's why it's called a *game*, isn't it? But maybe you're lucky, cos know what they say . . . a pessimist is never disappointed!'

'What the hell are you going on about? Anyway, I had a colleague who—' started Keith

'What the fuck's a *colleague?* A fucking *colleague?* Was this *colleague* a friend, or a work mate? No-one says fucking *colleague.* Jesus!' Tom was on the offensive, still laughing, but getting back at his drinking buddy.

'A colleague, co-worker, whatever. So this guy was a crazy football nut, used to go on all the coach trips for away-games and stuff, and one time there was this bird in the pub in Leeds, I think, and she was off her face, completely fucked. She got so wasted that she conked out early doors about seven that evening, slumped at the table. Royally fucked. Anyway, to cut a long story short, my *colleague*' – he emphasized the word theatrically – 'only went and got her black eyeliner out of her handbag, drew a bloody great swastika on her cheek and wrote S L A G on her forehead! She was only young, like seventeen or something, and when she woke up we sent her back to her mum and dad's house. Fuckin' hell, it was a rum affair!'

The men laughed disgracefully like hyenas and tugged on their beers, soon dispatching yet another can each into the recycling bag.

'I need to piss,' declared Keith. Tom replied with directions. 'The downstairs bog is blocked, so go upstairs if you can make it, and if there's a bed in the room then you're in the wrong place!'

Keith didn't know it, but Tom had a system for measuring *blokeishness*, mainly based of his perverse pride in being a raving alcoholic. It was a simple measurement, based on how much a man drank, combined with an estimate of how many shovel-loads of sand, dirt, or rubble Tom estimated that the guy had shifted in his life. He had mentally awarded Keith a score of around 60 Shovels (a figure out of 100), due to the fact that he could drink professionally, but didn't seem like the type to have carried out much hard manual work. Several of his hard hooligan mates back in the UK nudged the 90 Shovels mark, but he still tolerated Keith despite his mediocre Shovel rating, and sometimes the pair of them had a laugh getting pissed up together. Sue would be back soon and she would not be impressed . . .

Tom and Sue's neighbours were a bizarre set of people, yet typical of any local village in that area of France. The Bearded Lady painted a fine picture of rural life, and proudly displayed her tooth when she generously flashed a smile for the lucky recipient. It stood alone and prominent, and was very probably the only one left. Located in the middle of her mouth on the top deck, the last remaining tooth seemed perfectly poised for extracting snails from their shells, or scooping oysters up with ease. Equally as strange was the situation with her husband. He was always whistling tunelessly, but still managed to be a thoroughly miserable sod, and had unavoidably been forced to give up his profession as a roofer a number of years previously due to blindness. This information Tom and Sue had heard directly from his son, as well as on the local village grapevine. On one occasion, after Tom had shouted out a friendly 'Bonjour!' in the local town market, Monsieur Bearded Lady could clearly not focus on where the sound had come from, nor see who had accosted him, despite Tom and Sue's proximity. Still, the blind man was often spotted by Tom and Sue driving his ancient grey Citroën 'H-type' van around, sometimes on main roads at some speed. They could only imagine that the Bearded Lady was well-versed in the Art of Fine Directions when it came to driving, and that the man who always sported 1970s sunglasses behind the wheel remembered the roads well enough to navigate, as he had grown up and lived in the same village for his entire life like so many of the locals. He nearly always wore his black fingerless gloves, perhaps relics from his roofing days. In the cold winters of the countryside, the deeply penetrating chill numbed the bare tips of his fingers. He would pull deeply on his cigarette as if it somehow warmed him up, the particles of smoke embedding themselves into the 96% acrylic, 3% polyester and 1% elastic thread mix of his left glove, adding to its familiar man-hum.

Tom and Sue's typically short neighbour on the other side, Jean-Michel, was from one of those aristo-big-house-but-no-money kind of families. He and his long-suffering wife had come over for lunch one weekend not long after they had arrived to live in the village. Just as the main course was served and as the discussion turned to the local countryside, Jean-Michel launched into a lengthy tirade about the nearby lake, ranting about how he couldn't bear to go there as it was the chosen location of his brother's suicide thirty years previously. The unfortunate victim had taken himself up there with a loaded shotgun and a bottle of Pastis – not a winning combination, especially if depressed. The deed was done that balmy June evening, the shot reverberating around the surrounding countryside scattering birds from trees and sending rabbits scurrying into their dens. Meaningless but polite small talk seemed to have gone out of the window, and Tom – who was now pretty much at a loss for words – just about managed to bravely utter an optimistic 'Bon Appetit!'

The local town was fairly pretty, yet deathly quiet for most of the year, and the local area hosting quite a number of English couples and families. Stern middle-aged expensive-ly-dressed French ladies with brightly-coloured glasses and short red hair met with elegant men who wandered around with exclusive though gaudy cashmere jumpers draped over their shoulders. These coiffed fellows in their pastel colours and comfortable leather shoes, sporting cravats, were in the main *not* homosexual, but they managed to somehow carry a slight gay air about them that was particularly European. Perhaps some were, however, occasional or experimental homos, even if their wives had no clue about it; some almost cheating on their lovers with their wives. A fine boulangerie hugged the corner of the square alongside a deserted hotel. There didn't appear to be a large number of dogs about, but there was – proportionally – an inexplicable amount of dog shit littered about the pavements in the most unobvious places, apparently set up by the animal's owners as tourist booby traps. This, along with the suddenly-inflated prices in the cafés and bars once the hoards of pond-life tourists flock into the overrun centre in the summer, was what created memories of French summer holidays for so many English holidaymakers.

The farm was just up the track, with several inhumanely-caged hunting dogs ready to burst into an annoying fracas of barking at the slightest hint of a visitor. The poor mutts thrashed about incoherently in their own mess. Tom was clueless that Claude the farmer had been providing his wife with a little more than the occasional box of prime leeks or kindly bag or two of walnuts. His hair was longish, yet very organized, maybe like Action Man were he a hippy. Chunky bracelet matched heavy medallion, always hanging proudly, which was framed by one in a line of Claude's denim shirts, always open a few inches too low. His face displayed a life of outdoor work, a gentle contentment radiated from his being and Sue found him irresistibly charming. Claude had, in fact, been proudly flying the flag for France and her tradition of secret, or even blatantly-public affairs for married 50-something men. The unlikely scene was set one typically sultry summer's evening when Tom and Sue had been invited for aperitifs at the farmhouse. Any slight hints of social awkwardness at the outset rapidly melted as the locally-produced drink flowed freely, with Claude's natural exuberance and hospitality soon putting everyone at ease. Not unexpectedly, the party soon developed into an extended bender of a drinking session with much laughter and frivolity, the very picture of l'entente cordiale complete with a good spattering of franglais. Claude ended up driving Tom and Sue back sometime after midnight, and the events that followed can only be described as fairly bizarre.

On arriving home, Tom clumsily stumbled out of Claude's rusty but trusty Renault, disappearing through the front door just about able to manage a subdued, 'Yeah, a bit of careful drink-driving never hurt anyone, I suppose! Merci, bon nuit.' The car's motor came to an abrupt halt and Claude and Sue were surprised by the sudden silence of the countryside night. Sue managed to turn her head to violently vomit out of the passenger-seat window, spattering much of the door as well as depositing an impressive multi-coloured pool of alcoholic mess on the courtyard gravel. No sooner had she wiped her mouth with her sleeve and managed to open the door to pull herself up on her feet, than Claude appeared out of the night to launch himself earnestly at her, swiftly thrusting his rude and eager tongue into her stinking mouth. Exact memories blurred for her at this stage, but she remained fairly sure that it was all over in a matter of seconds. This was the version that she convinced herself of, anyway. Somewhere there was a hazy recollection of pushing the farmer away and turning into the shadows of the house, somewhere a muddy memory of the amazing embarrassed whirring sound that only old cars can make. Although the following day she awoke and was at first shocked as it all hit her abruptly through the harrowing fog of her hangover, she soon grew to appreciate the excitement in the dangerous prospect of having an ongoing illicit liaison with the Frenchman. This was exactly what lay ahead in her Destiny – she knew deep down, and it was now down to just the finer details of when and how exactly it would come about . . .

Paul shuffled around the back room of his musty antique shop in Acton, west London, unenthusiastically reorganizing a box of 1970s pornography and moving a creepy stash of Nazi memorabilia from under the stuffed owl to his counter top where he was planning to have a rifle through it that afternoon. These were the kinds of specialist items that were kept discreetly a little more out of sight, with the front room displaying a far more conservative range of traditional antiques, oddities and rarities. He was a mad James Bond fan, so had an area dedicated to his personal collection, despite the items not being up for sale. Regrettably, he himself lacked any of the charisma and personal style of Bond, but owned however some rare and quite valuable collectable items from the 007 franchise. The once-elegant building had seen better days, and the intended re-decoration that he occasionally planned always got postponed or forgotten about. Discoloured wallpaper peeled and hung sadly from the corners of the front room, and ominous-looking yet delicate black mould spores occupied an ever-increasing area around the chilled window frames. Chet Baker's impossibly melancholic tones drifted casually out of some ageing speakers, as an eclectic mix of people of all ages, races and upbringings drifted past on the pavement, barely even glancing at the lovingly-collected range of artefacts on display in the window. Paul had a keen eye for pieces of all types, with years of experience behind him and many contacts in the game. His clients came from far and wide to see him, all the more so as he had point-blank refused to modernize by photographing and displaying his artefacts on the web as the vast majority of his competitors were doing. It was his old-school style and doggedness that actually endeared him to many of his buyers, especially the older ones. Despite the constant drizzle of rain outside, the day had presented him with a fairly decent sale by late morning, and his mood was relatively upbeat for a change. Overbearing and ugly plastic glasses perched dubiously on the bridge of his bulbous nose, their frame too thick for his face, their nondescript colour too dark for his complexion. Rubbery oversized earlobes swung slightly as he spun on his heels to see who was at the door, and the ugly wiry hairs protruded aggressively out of his nostrils, interfering disrespectfully with the airspace that they invaded, occasionally brushing the blackheads which dotted the flaring side flaps of his nose. Then out of the blue Tony breezed in confidently, flashing an expensive smile at Paul, and an outstretched hand. Just behind him blew in a waft of booze and fags. 'Hello, old friend, long time no see,' the unexpected visitor chirped melodiously.

It had, indeed, been quite some time since the two men had seen each other, a good ten years. The event had been a mutual friend's funeral, and his untimely death had been a bit of a shock to both men as they were the same age as the deceased. Somewhat oddly, it was also the day that Paul met his third and current wife. She too had been attending to pay her respects, being a work colleague of the dead man.

The bittersweet irony of the fact that they had met and come together due to the sad demise of a friend in common had not gone unnoticed, with the couple often thanking him with a toast aimed skywards in his memory. 'Here's to you, Bernard you ol' bastard!' they would chirp, laughing, before gulping down another impolitely-full beaker of just-drinkable red wine.

Paul involuntarily stepped back briefly in his surprise, recognizing Tony at once. Then a bone-crushing handshake followed, Tony the Crusher.

'Well, well – look who it is! Wonders never cease to amaze me. Come on in, Tony, you don't look a day over, well . . . forty, shall we say?'

The familiar and cliché-rich banter kicked off as the two men realised that neither one had changed enormously in the ten years since they'd last seen each other. Paul couldn't help but notice Tony's blatantly obvious blond hair-dye effort, and mentally remarked that it made him look fairly ridiculous – the man in his mid to late sixties clearly clutching at straws in some feeble effort to retain some essence of his youth (all the more so when combined with the shiny face and impossibly white gnashers). Before too long – but not before he had managed to sell Tony a beautiful old map of India for his study wall – the shop would be shut for the afternoon. Paul's premises looked drab and forlorn as the CLOSED sign swung gently against the murky glass in the door, the filthy and ugly metal shutters sliding down to keep vandals and would-be burglars at bay. It was the start of the afternoon and too early to start drinking really, but this out-of-the-blue surprise called for a pint or two.

'Beverage? Boozer, perhaps?' Paul proposed with a smile.

'Does a bear shit in the woods? C'mon!'

Most people were out at work at this hour, which left the pavement generally quiet but for the odd granny, dosser or mum with pram. 'Ah, the most honest weather in the world,' remarked Tony as they set off down the street in the drizzle, stepping around a pile of black household rubbish bags piled carelessly at the base of a tree.

The Pig & Whistle was all but deserted when they strolled in and sat near the open fire to enjoy a livener. A cold local gardener appeared to be fixed to the bar, throwing a pint of strong lager down his neck between mundane jobs, his nose that of a seasoned alcoholic dripping constantly like a tap in need of a new washer. At a manly safe distance away was perched a portly Asian guy with sides of head shaved, his fluorescent T-shirt proclaiming that he was 'Single and Disease-Free'. He was nursing a tomato juice. An third anonymous person was alone at a table for six, *reading A Pilgrim in Paradise* by A. P. Nest, never looking up. Tony supped gingerly at the first pint of beer, and immediately pulled a face like a puppy licking a stinging nettle. By the second slurp, however, his taste buds had come around to appreciating the guest ale.

'I was on the way to the office in Henley-on-Thames, walking through the park yesterday. It's all very pleasant, all a bit twee, you see . . . even the old people smell nice! There are the posh parents shouting things like 'Alfie, take that stick out of Jasper's eyeball now . . . I'll count to three!' or 'Phoebe, extract your index finger from your brother's bottom this instant!' No gangs or chavs, well, not too many anyway. So I get there, the office, and have this key that must have been kicking around in my desk for maybe seven years, and I've only just stumped up the courage to chuck it out. Seven long years. Throwing old keys away has got to be one of the hardest things to do, don't you find Paul? Well I do. I've no idea what the bloody thing was for and it's unlikely I'll ever bloody remember. It's still making me feel a bit . . . you know, *uncomfortable*, though – it could have been for something important.' Tony could chat, but at least he wasn't short on wit.

'Sounds sort of Biblical, you know, the whole seven years lark. But still, don't worry yourself mate, it was probably just the Key to Life!' Paul consoled his old friend. Tony then tried to persuade Paul that the Welsh word for carrot is *moron*, but Paul wasn't having it. It dawned on him later that he hadn't had such a laugh in far too long. Halfway through the third pint though Tony turned uncharacteristically serious, having a moan about Norman and Polly, getting some concerns off his chest and vaguely touching on the terms that he had laid out to them back at the restaurant. Paul listened, looking suitably reflective.

'Enough about my difficult children anyway,' Tony carried on, suddenly aware that he was probably boring Paul.

'Well, you know I managed to give up smoking a few years back?' Paul was talking quietly all of a sudden, forcing to Tony listen in. 'It was weird, I had my ear pierced, something I've always half-meant to do since I was young, and the guy that did it, he touched something . . . I can't quite explain, but he touched something that changed me. Ever since he pierced my ear, I never touched a cigarette again. I've never wanted to. Very strange. The dreams about a giant cigarette hot air balloon were a bit out there, too.'

Tony paused in reflection, before asking, 'Yep, but I bet you keep fit now and feel better for it?'

'Well, how can you *keep* fit if you were never fit in the first place? I don't get it when I see some fat unhealthy person saying that they're off to *keep* fit, it should be called *get* fit! And no, I feel exactly as I did when I was chuffing away, except that I can smell things better now. But that goes for bad stinks as well as the pleasant stuff, so it's not always a good thing. It's like when I was in Africa recently, you know, a little holiday – it turned out to be more interesting than fun, though. The smells were incredible, markets, spices, you know . . . good stuff. And the hotel was so beautiful and luxurious it just made you wanna do something illegal! I just got a bit freaked when I heard that there was a ban on the polio eradication programme by extreme Islamists in nearby Nigeria, which led to outbreaks in about twenty neighbouring countries. I never had the sugar cube inoculation when I was a kid, or since, so I came back a bit early. Then as I had a bit of free time still, I went up to the Yorkshire Moors, but it turned out to be a long weekend of fog – I did a bloody 1,000-piece puzzle of a cat in front of a bookshelf, damn nightmare! It was supposed to be all walking and reading but ended up being all drinking, sleeping and puzzling!'

Tony frowned, then they laughed, easily relaxed in each other's company after such a long time. Tony explained how he'd gone to a mid-afternoon film recently, and that, as he was all alone in the cinema, he didn't turn off his phone.

'Yeah, it felt good. I was a rebel with my phone on in the cinema, ringer on full volume, no problem. In fact, I was a bit annoyed that nobody called!'

Paul studied his old friend, thinking that age had not been too unkind to him. Tony, on the other hand, was amazed to observe how rough-looking Paul had become since their last meeting. He particularly noticed the unnatural-looking and aggressively-sprouting ginger hairs like tiny wires that matted the back of Paul's hand and spindly fingers, whose neglected nails harboured ten different ecosystems of grime and matter. As if on cue, these very nails suddenly tapped out a majestic rhythm on the table, as though concluding a certain topic of conversation.

Tony lurched slightly as he stood up from the table. 'I've just got to go for a slash. D'you know, I seem to spend the bulk of my waking life these days either looking for somewhere to take a piss or seeking out some liquid to drink! Look, there's too much air in your glass, I'll get another one on my way back.'

He found himself leaning his bulky frame over the urinal to steady himself. 'Shit, it stinks like the inside of a tramp's handbag in here!' he muttered, glancing up at some informative biro-scrawled graffiti on the wall: *Julia Cast is a slag.* Underneath someone had replied with a different pen: *I know, she sucked me off and swallowed.* Tony chortled as he carefully zipped up.

The moment he was back at the table the chat carried on. 'I thought I'd come and see you and ask you over to the golf club for a bit of a knock around, you know. You were always pretty mean with the irons back in the day, I remember. Maybe around the end of the month we'll get down there . . . jump on the train so we can have a bevvy afterwards, what d'you think?' And so it was agreed, and the two men managed another couple of pints together before setting out into the night to stumble their separate ways.

Will bounded down the steep steps out of the mansion block

near Fulham Broadway and almost fell out of the doorway. A sudden brightness in the morning light hit him and the spiteful breath of the icy wind burnt his cheek. He almost collided with a flustered and rather stout sweaty runner who he was only 85% sure was female, but his breezy 'Sorry!' was only met with a disapproving scowl. Feeling glad to be alive this particular day, he had woken in the right frame of mind (all sunshine, lollipops and rainbows!), which certainly was not always the case. His compact cat had been lying neatly on top of him, intently staring at him. 'Well I dunno about you, Pat, but I slept like a baby last night. Although, having said that, I've never quite got that expression as babies quite often wake up at 3 a.m. and cause havoc . . . but you slept well, I hope?' The cat didn't reply. Pat's full name was Pat the Transexual Cat because when Will first had her, he was convinced that it was a male. After a perfunctory examination by the vet, however, Will was informed that Patrick needed to become Patricia. At least it was no problem with the name, so Pat remained Pat.

Through the haze of his waking moments, Will's first decision of the day was to have a staring match with Pat, with the loser being the first to look away. He shifted around in the bed, finding an area of refreshingly cool pillow to prop himself up somewhat, preparing for the ultimate battle. An entire two minutes passed before Pat slowly closed her eyes and settled down to sleep. 'Yes!' Will exclaimed, glad to be in a winning mood today as he forced himself up to jump out of bed, sending Pat dashing out of the bedroom door. The golden standard of sleep – eight hours – had been relished. A wide Victorian tap spluttered into life in the bathroom as Will waited 20 seconds for the hot H_2O to flow. He scrubbed his teeth and rinsed with hot water, an old habit; he believed they cleaned better hot. A breakfast of scrambled eggs and lemonade was almost bouncing in his belly as he ran down the steps to the Underground platform. He chuckled as he passed a Winkworth Estate Agent's *SOLD* sign outside a grotty flat that some clever soul had scrawled 'Thank Christ you're leaving!' onto, and in a different pen was agreed with, with a simple 'Yeh!' An old track from Kid Creole and the Coconuts blasted from a window somewhere above, and Will dug it. Unusual for music to be played at a decent volume at this hour, he thought. Will was generally a very relaxed guy, in fact he was so *chilled out* that his demeanour sometimes annoyed people. He had been described as a 'humid day' by an ex-girlfriend, but never did really grasp what she was getting at. Suddenly his pocket beeped twice. He pulled out a battered mobile phone and stabbed at a button or two. A text from his best mate Mark:

> *Am at Gatwick en route 4 Amsterdam. 7 or 8 highly pokeable Dutch birds here, 2 of them nudging 10/10. It's horrible. Where can one get chemically castrated?*

Will grinned as the train rumbled down the vintage tracks into the station. He negotiated his way onto the carriage, sitting next to a pleasantly plump Polish-looking girl who appeared to be under assault from her mp3 player's tinny pop music, polluting the immediate surrounding area unapologetically, as well as her brain. It seemed that she was one of many who liked music that's produced for people who don't like music. He vaguely recognized the song, but it certainly didn't sound as good as he remembered as it leaked out of her headphones, the repetition sending him into a mild trance as he stared unthinking out of the window. A shifty character with an unacceptable haircut – whose face looked like it had been pushed into a wall many years ago – stood by the door refusing to put down a brown box that he clasped into his side as the train rattled along. *Handel with care* had been scribbled onto a green sticker on the box's side, and he thought that old George Frideric would have been fairly amused by this in his own Baroque manor. An oddly-shaped female of indeterminate age wore a vacant expression – was she actually an idiot or was it just a sign of extreme boredom? Her sinister make-up caught his eye as she splurged out a mighty cough. This caused her ample spongy bosom to morph into her ample spongy belly on the forward lean, tiny fat hand barely covering podgy mouth, her general mass disgusting him somewhat (although surely appealing to certain males . . . or perhaps not?). She could be 25, or maybe 48? Her bright neck scarf must be an attempt to cover some of the offensive mass, or at least distract from it. On his right the obligatory spotty youth sucked on a dry, salty pork pie as small pieces dropped to the floor, brow deeply furrowed and greedy eyes squinting in concentration, or possibly uncertainty in the enjoyment of the snack. Next to him sat an unlikely character, faded tattoo (of a swallow, was it?) a couple of centimetres long, barely protruding from his shirt collar. The same shirt cupped his mini pot belly, a silver ring dangled uselessly from his earlobe, and wet-look gel was streaked liberally through his thinning hair, like a storm-soaked marshland. All these people! Will found himself pondering where to find a piano tuner for the beaten-up upright that his grandma had recently left to him. He was considering calling the RNIB. Weren't blind people supposed to be the best piano tuners? An awkwardly sexy young woman opposite him with grapefruit cheeks suddenly reminded him of someone, but he couldn't place who. The more he admired her, the more her feline features drew him in. He studied her thick and extraordinary waterproof 70s porn green mascara until she suddenly held his gaze and scowled at him – he realised that he'd possibly scared her with his intense scrutiny, so hurriedly raised his eyes to an advert for *vitamins for pregnant women* above her head. Thoughts turned to the day ahead. As a struggling session guitarist doing gigs and scraps of recording – mainly around London – Will had recently reached the stage at which he'd accept pretty much anything in the way of work. He felt that he'd been scratching around for too long, and had even lately taken on three adult guitar students, although he hated teaching.

Only the previous weekend he had begrudgingly driven up to Edinburgh in a rusty old Post Office van with a tribute band to The Jam that he played in from time to time. They could barely nudge 55mph all the way and were crammed in with the scratched up flight cases and gear. After almost ten hours driving and nearly sick with crisps, sweets and biscuits, they eventually stumbled upon the venue which was a floating club on a dimly lit boat that had seen better days. The singer dropped down the short flight of steps from the manager's office looking deflated. 'All the bastard posters and flyers that we sent the twat a month ago are sat on a pile on the edge of his desk. There's gonna be nobody there.' And for a change, he was right. No-one came, and after they'd played half-heartedly for an hour, the manager told them to go home. At around 11 p.m. that night, the band of four young men, all with £75 pay in their pocket, set off for the 10-hour overnight journey home.

'Well, that was shit.' Baz was precise, and as if the situation required some sort of explanation, he added, 'You know what Adam Ant said? He said that 'being a musician is like being a boxer: if you don't want to get punched in the face every day then this job isn't for you.' Well I think he might just have a point there.'

The weirdest gig that he'd ever done was at a chair museum, but today that achievement was about to take second place to something even odder. His drummer mate Dave had somehow secured a series of educational concerts, consisting of a sporadic tour around a number of prisons starting in the south of England. They had rehearsed sketchily the day before at a wretched flea-bitten and cheap studio tucked under some railway arches, and Will was now en route to the agreed pick-up spot where the guys and all the gear would be ready in a van for the drive to Highcrest Prison, Suffolk. The general sentiment among the musicians was slight disbelief that someone in a position of power thought it a reasonable expense to the taxpayer for this band of young music-makers to be performing to inmates in any prison. It was triumph for Political Correctness, and the men – and women, of course – in suits would have garbled all the right words to justify reasons for the booking, citing *therapy* and *rehabilitation*. They were even talking about giving prisoners internet access too. What next: £100 vouchers for Ikea and a weekly coach trip there for meatballs? Still, they were getting handsomely rewarded and Dave remained happy with himself for securing this deal that looked like a possible ongoing gig for the group.

'Why can't we be called Maidenhead or something? It's kinda a cross between Iron Maiden and Motörhead. Or maybe even Leatherhead? It gives us that funky bondage edge, you know?' Dave joked.

'How about Guildford?' questioned Baz, tentatively. 'Or something like Wasted Erection?' Laughter.

For the remainder of the drive the guys entertained themselves by devising novel and disgusting drinks, named after old-skool British 'celebrities'. The following unlikely menu of beverages was dreamt up:

JIM DAVIDSON: double Baileys with a double vodka, no ice, served in a wine glass, preferably on a ferry

FELICITY KENDALL: vodka & Red Bull

KEITH CHEGWIN: a Felicity Kendall with Champagne

GARY WILMOTT: gin & any alcopop, no ice

MICK HUCKNALL: half pint of Carling shandy, perhaps a little warm

JIMMY SAVILE: vanilla ice cream diet Coke float with an umbrella, liberally splashed with Malibu, and a sprinkling of Smarties

NOEL EDMONDS: vodka & Pepto-Bismol

SANDI TOKSVIG: Crème de Menthe & lime cordial

CRAIG DAVID: Canada Dry & whisky, with a thin slice of lemon and a drizzle of honey, preferably served with a lit sparkler

ANT & DEC: just salt & lime, no tequila, × 2

It had been decided by the prison authorities that for the purpose of their UK tour, the group would be named The Prison Breakers. These dutiful Civil Servants viewed themselves as being very modern and forward-thinking for proposing and permitting this entire venture, especially with their humorous choice of band name, but Dave and the band hated it. That was that, though, and the musicians had no choice in the matter. They were a typically funny bunch of London-based musos, the odd group of disparate young guys searching for a place in the world of bands around town. The sullen bass player Baz seemed continually depressed and was constantly putting up barriers. This could have been for two reasons, and Will for one certainly couldn't figure out which one it was: either Baz was fairly dumb so felt out of his depth, or it was a sign of genuine ennui and a hugely outwardly-apparent sign of general disappointment with life. He had certainly passed the point of feeling young and still expecting something out of life. At least he spoke from time to time, which was more to be said for T the singer, who – unusually for a front man – barely uttered a word off stage. He had nearly had a huge career (like so many others), having been signed with his Indie band The Normals for a laughably large sum to a major label a few years previously. It had all gone pear-shaped, though (like so many others), and generally he had caned and spanked himself with drugs (like so many others), and now spent most of the time caring for his elderly and increasingly cantankerous mother in Liverpool. They even had a pretty comprehensive rider, on which, aside from the usual array of alcohol and snacks, was listed:

6 × Men's pants, an assortment of sizes
Some Lego & Airfix kits
Local postcards, with stamps
Aloe Vera toilet rolls
6 packets of Malboro Lights, and a brick containing
Swan Vesta matches
10 × £10 notes, crisp
Male facial moisturiser
A copy of the *New Scientist*, and *Viz*
3 × pencils and a metal sharpener
A bottle of Calvin Klein CK One
A USB lead
Mini Thesaurus

So where were the rest of The Normals?

'Bareback' Len, guitarist, born 26-09-81, in Cardiff. Got a girl pregnant in Cleveland, Ohio, on the band's one and only professionally disastrous but hugely entertaining promotional trip to the States. Disappeared back over there after record label dropped them to set up new life with her on her trailer park. Tried to punt his demo CD *Unsigned, Sealed and Delivered* by his newly-formed punk outfit Lemon Layer Pudding around various record labels and managers, but unsurprisingly nobody wanted to know. Hasn't been seen or heard of since.

Favourite food: Pringles.

Quote: 'It's a beautiful thing.'

Derek 'What U Lookin' At?', drummer, born Bristol, 03-05-79. Got massively shafted by the Inland Revenue after some highly suspicious accounting submitted by his accountant friend who he'd met in the local pub. Had just found out that he got a groupie pregnant in Chicago on the band's one and only promotional trip to the States. Also around the same time, he realised that he was gay, and started taking even more drugs. A heady cocktail of guilt, confusion, hangovers and disappointment – merged with his brush with fame – lead to his tragic end. He unfortunately jumped off the famous suicide bridge onto the A1 in North London one sunny Tuesday morning after a particularly heavy weekend. He'd watched Frank Sinatra in Can-Can on the Monday afternoon, and one quote rang and rebounded around his head until one of the options made nothing but total sense to him whilst in that particular day's morbidly specific frame of mind: 'I've considered murder, suicide and chronic alcoholism . . .'

Favourite colour: yellow.

'Deaf-Aid' Mike, Bass player, born 01-12-84, somewhere in Somerset. Last known to be studying geology at an establishment in Copenhagen. Loves chilli, and once suffered a serious nosebleed backstage after eating a couple of small pieces of Bhut Jolokia, recognized as the hottest pepper in the world by the Guinness Book of Records in 2007. Favourite stunt on tour: shitting inside the front of hairdryers in hotel rooms, a present for the next user. Quotes: 'I slightly collapsed, well . . . I think I may have slightly collapsed . . .' and 'Did we get really pissed last night?'

Back in the near-glory days of their career they supported a band whose first album cost £40,000 to make and sold 1,000,000 copies, but whose second album cost £1,000,000 to make yet sold 40,000 copies. The day that their record label dropped them publicly was the day of the gig that the two bands did together at Norwich University. Still, even such a monumental disaster as this was almost a goal for The Normals. They once blagged a pretty decent slot mid-afternoon on one of the larger Glastonbury stages, but it had all gone wrong. They had driven down in a tour bus the day before the show with twelve bottles of vodka, a generous wrap of MDMA each, and far too many kilograms of meat. That night turned from messy to outrageous as they consumed all the drugs and heavily dented the vodka supply. Mike was Missing in Action the day of the show, and the rest of the group were too terrified to leave the bus, instead they sat sweating and shaking in fear on a heavy comedown. They never made it to the stage. Needless to say, the glistening pile of meat was never to see the grills of the barbecue which lay in its box shining to itself in the darkness, untouched.

People nowadays would be hard-pressed to notice the fact, but Will had suffered with severe mental problems a few years back. Once, after driving a stolen car in a straight line up Ladbroke Crescent thereby smashing into twenty or so cars (the geometry didn't work out), he uttered the immortal lines 'It's a fair cop, guv' to the arresting officer. The policeman was subsequently forced to repeat this in court, much to the amusement of those attending. This alone had generated huge respect from Mark who found this one of the funnier stories he'd ever heard.

Will was now much better and appeared these days to be out of the woods. It had all started after a particularly bad acid trip. He turned into a walking soap opera. After burning the only surviving picture of a friend's grandmother in the kitchen sink, 'because the coffee machine was haunted', he was picked up completely naked by Surbiton Constabulary after ringing the Ambulance Service from a public call box not far from the station at 6 a.m. one chilly Saturday morning. He was confused, rambling idiotically on his way to the police station, and although the number of words per minute spouting crazily out of his dry mouth soon diminished, the jumbled confusion in his brain continued. This incident and subsequent evaluations were to eventually lead to his incarceration in an imposing Victorian psychiatric hospital, surrounded by woods. Although his manner would become erratic and slightly crazed at times, he could equally often appear perfectly sane. The other unfortunate inmates were at varying stages of illness, and the general atmosphere was one of barely-controlled chaos.

'How's things, Will? Great to see you, mate. I've brought you some garibaldis and a bunch of grapes.' The grapes were a kind of ironic joke, but he knew that Will loved his Garibaldi biscuits. Mark had been led through to the secure wing where he found Will watching a gardening show on daytime TV – with the sound off.

'I'm strong,' Will replied simply, getting up from the worn and frayed armchair.

'Let me show you the two Jesus guys. It's weird, you know, there are these two geezers who are both convinced that they are the Second Coming of Jesus, and d'you know what the crazy wardens have done? They've put them both in a tiny padded room together so they can battle it out! How mad is that!? You've got to check it out!' So Will led Mark down a bright corridor to show him the two men in a room together, one huddled up in a corner and the other just sitting, staring at the wall. They both had bushy beards and longish hair, but there appeared to be no contact between the Jesus men as Mark peered in inquisitively. They hung around outside the room for a while but disappointingly it appeared that there was no matinee performance from the two *Sons of God* this particular afternoon. Mark couldn't suppress a chuckle at the unusual set-up.

A short while later and without any warning Will became excited like a small child and ran across to the wall, gleefully smashing glass to set off the fire alarm, showing off with a jumpy manner Mark hadn't witnessed in him before. After laughing strangely and madly for a few minutes, Will quietly admitted to one of the staff with a cheeky old-fashioned wink that the alarm had been set off by him. Becoming angry and upset after being mildly reprimanded, the situation rapidly turned ugly, and before long there were several hassled nurses bundling him onto the floor, restraining him then marching him off down a long corridor. Mark's visit had been abruptly cut short. He had seen enough of the place by this time anyway; it was the kind of horrendous establishment that he had no idea still existed in quite such an antiquated form in the UK, and he felt more than just a little uncomfortable there. What the fuck was that hideously ugly and imposing bust of Beethoven doing in the entrance hall anyway? The entire hospital conjured up scenes that were remarkably close to *One Flew Over the Cuckoo's Nest,* and he had been particularly disturbed although not unamused after seeing one patient in the art block lying on a sofa in his dressing-gown suddenly start to furiously masturbate and emit a weird walrus-like noise as a female member of staff swiftly scuttled by. What he would never know was that Colin was a serial masturbator, whose desultory actions never enhanced his life: doing this many times a day, feeling no emotion, becoming neither happier nor more depressed, more tired or awake. It was his direction in life.

'Over here, friend, over here,' beckoned a wiry, friendly-looking character. 'If gay's your way then that's okay . . .' Mark shook his head slowly, holding his gaze. 'I've got to tell you something important, seriously, you've got to hear me.' The man was at Mark's elbow now, frowning. Mark smiled wryly at something written clearly and neatly on the wall in felt tip above the guy's head: *neverbeensectioned.com*

He took his time. 'It's ketchup. It makes me cross. Really cross. I get angry at the sight of it, its unnecessary redness, its artificial smell . . . the vinegar. And what winds me right up, my friend, is that everyone always assumes that you'll like it, that it's universally adored, that you want it ruining and staining your food. Well, I'm going to let you into a little secret – they're wrong! Not everyone likes ketchup . . . I mean, look at me, I HATE IT! Can't stand the vile jelly-like putrid fake matter. Soggy ketchup-ridden chips, absolutely disgusting.' The incensed man paused for breath. 'Absolutely fucking dis-gust-ing!' He almost spat out the words. 'Some people are even rude enough to put it on your food.' He pulled a face.

'What, not even on the side of the plate or whatever? It *does* have certain properties, you know,' taunted Mark, rather enjoying himself now.

'Listen, friend.' Mr Ketchup lowered his voice conspiratorially while leaning forward a little. 'If it's put anywhere near your food, you can get nasty seepage or cross-contamination. It can be dangerous, you mark my words, it can be very dangerous.' Mr Ketchup straightened himself up all of a sudden. His face relaxed, revealing deep furrows around his taut mouth. 'Well, great to meet you, friend. Don't forget!'

And with that he turned and marched away, leaving Mark wincing from some particularly rank fallout in the surrounding atmosphere from his meaty breath.

Mark also witnessed a line of weedy ill-kempt men shuffling pathetically along in a line to receive their medication at what looked like an ice-cream van window. One of them, with a horrible beard and a stripy T-shirt, had a tattoo on his forearm stating *Only God Can Judge Me*. The rosary decoration surrounding it didn't improve it in any way. He was almost squealing at the male nurse behind the grill, 'Haven't you got any damn Q-Tips? I'm sure I had some about fifteen years ago, but I can't remember where they are! God dammit!'

Will had lucidly explained that, although it all looked fairly regulated and they had to pop it back or drink it in front of a nurse, the medication was somehow regularly stashed away and traded between the patients. Lots of these already fragile people were often ingesting and swallowing alarmingly bizarre cocktails of antipsychotic drugs about which they had no idea, which often weren't even destined for them. How anybody could ever actually improve and get better in such a place was baffling Mark, and as he drifted around he felt as if he had become yet another player on the stage that was the ward, feeling surreally not connected to Real Life. The spirit of the place was clearly rubbing off on him, and he wondered ruefully how long some of the patients (or were they inmates?) had been there.

He heard random snapshots of conversation throughout the afternoon, and, although fascinating, the madness was exhausting:

'. . . and then the girl said that I wasn't in Poundland, I was in Poundworld, and that Poundland was over the other side, but that I had nothing to worry about because prices were generally very similar . . . but if they had a 10% sale would it become the 90p shop?'

And, in a very posh deep voice, '. . . so the late-night randoms were all there (including yours truly), a large cast including the usual small-fry drug pushers, a racist homosexual, and a 68-year-old gran who I very nearly took home to my bed . . . all a little off their faces, of course, if that's possible . . . well, in fact I suppose being off your face has to be by its very nature an all-consuming state but . . . '

And: '. . . and the crab omelette, fuck me, it was nothing like the bleedin' picture . . . all chive garnish, givin' it all the tomato salad this 'n' that on the side with the juicy crab meat bursting out of the side. Nah, it was like a fackin' flat pancake with a bit of tinned fackin' crab wetting up the side. Shit. He said I could take it up with the chef if I wanted. 'Is he big?' I asked him. 'No, he's small,' was the reply . . .'

There were more, although many were silent: 'How I haven't been sent down is one enormous mystery to me, but it must be down to a good accent and the ability to scrub up well. Clean-shaven and sporting cufflinks, expensive polished shoes and ironed shirts, one can fool lots of people a lot of the time . . .'

'. . . don't do it, no, not now, no please! You can't. Don't do it, I beg you, there's no need, no . . ! You remind me of my tortoise that went into hibernation but never came out again. Then I was annoyed with my mother because I was away, and she'd gone and buried the damn thing and wouldn't tell me where, but I'd wanted to use the shell as an ashtray!'

'. . . she asked me to move the Head and Shoulders out of view in the bathroom, saying that everyone would know that I've got dandruff. I told her no, cos everyone will know that I *haven't* got dandruff because I use Head and Shoulders!' and '. . . yeah, and him and the Mrs hadn't had sex for two years, they go to Glastonbury and do a pill, get jiggy in the tent only to end up with a second kid out of the blue!'

'. . . so we're in this shabby but incredible French château talking *politics* with the oysters and champagne, *literature* with the rare lamb, *cheese* with the cheese, then the *irony and difficulty of spending one's existence in permanent debt* with the strawberries. All conversation and food of course washed down with exquisite Bordeaux from a decanter, while outside monsters masquerading as fish were devouring everything that their google-eyes spotted in the murky moat which surrounded the place. The batty owner, an aging German-French widow of a famous writer from the 80s, still offering her recovering alcoholic daughter wine – jeez – 'just a drop to be convivial,' she'd say. And the daughter, still clearly fragile many years later, replying wearily as if this was a well-rehearsed act, 'Mother, you still appear to forget that I was a drug addict from the age of 15 to 21, and then an alcoholic to the age of 30, and still . . . ,' and the mother would just laugh. But the peppermill, what an item! A grossly phallic brass and frankly ugly object from Delphi, Greece, weighty at that . . .'

He had to snap out of this frame of mind, or he would simply become one of *them*, merging in, perhaps eventually finding a bed to sleep in, then robotically getting up to queue up at the kiosk window for his drugs, ready to start the day with all the others . . .

Afternoon tea had been served out of a slightly chipped oddly-patterned cup and saucer that reminded Mark of village halls. Will was convinced that there were turquoise patches of mould on the sponge cakes, and that the milk had 'turned', neither of which were true as far as Mark could tell. He didn't eat or drink, having decided to talk at length, seizing the moment to recount tales about his sexual exploits with a polyphrenic girl who he would regularly meet on a moss-covered roof near the kitchen area. If she had on that particular day assumed her persona of Scary Donna, then she would hiss abuse at him, often being fairly spiteful and aggressive. She explained that she had been raped, had indulged in several threesomes and loved recreational drugs, also that she had attempted suicide on a number of occasions, most recently by locking herself inside a refrigeration truck full of eerie dangling meat carcasses. Having been discovered many hours later by the shocked driver, barely managing to cling onto life, she had become known as Donna the Fridge Magnet. When she was Donna, Will would humour her but not hang around for too long as her venomous insults had often been known to make him cry if he was having a fragile day. However, if she was indulging her Roxy persona, then very few words would pass between them, she would be all over him and they would enjoy dirty and sometimes curious sex. He found her intensely gorgeous, being especially drawn to the train tracks on her teeth and her slightly boss-eyed glare, so she was like a lamb to the slaughter. She remained biscuit-thin, whoever she was, and had a problem telling the truth. A biscuit hadn't passed her lips in several years. There were a couple of other occasions when they had met around the grounds by chance, and she had appeared to not recognise him at all. She was a hard one to crack, that's for sure, a fully fucked-up bunny. One day she had hit him pretty hard on the skull with a hairdryer in an attack that neither of them could fully understand afterwards. All of this presumably meant that there were other characters inside her head too, and not all of them had yet encountered Will. He was never sure if he ever found out her real name . . .

'But you see, life *can* be a like bowl of cherries, even with a cherry on top . . . I even get laid in a place like this!' Will exclaimed, flapping his arms around at the surrounding building. Some heads turned, only to look away.

'Yeah, it's not all bad,' agreed Mark, encouragingly. 'We've all got our own problems, in here or out in the 'normal' world. I mean, for instance, I've got an ugly big toe.'

'Well, yeah, you're right. You know, my cat's got bad breath, really something,' added Will.

'My cousin's got AIDS, and I like to talk to my banana tree.'

'Well . . . my mother never speaks to me.'

The game continued. Mark's turn.

'I bought *Philosophy for Dummies* recently and haven't opened it yet. Who buys that?! Hold on, worse still, I had skid marks in my boxer shorts last week!'

'I get nervous in crowds,' replied Will after laughing briskly.

Mark: 'I'm rubbish at spelling and I can't stand dirty cutlery.'

Now Will decided to up the challenge. 'I have a recurring dream; I think it's really a fantasy of mine. I end up raping a chicken, and the chicken actually starts to enjoy it!'

'Jeez, are you normal or paranormal? Ok, well, you've got me there!' Mark conceded, grinning broadly.

Will also described a doctor who he had been seeing every Monday morning, and it all sounded rather odd. A certain Dr Watson who suffered from severe eczema and so wore white cotton gloves at all times as if she was at an early 90s acid rave. Her billowing Paisley-print Laura Ashley dresses confused the whole image, conjuring visions of a country mum. It seemed that it didn't really help seeing a psychiatric consultant who was like a freaky extra from the summer rave posse when you're trying to get better.

Following the incident with the fire alarm, Mark wasn't bothered about staying, but still he sad for Will, combined with a sensation of unreality and distortion of the world, the latter having presumably stemmed from spending a large part of the day in the company of nutters. Such depersonalization was certainly not a feeling he enjoyed, so he tried to clear his head on the stroll back to the station, wishing that he still smoked as it would have been the ideal moment to spark up. On the drearily slow train ride back to London, he forced his mind to think of his forthcoming holidays, and other pleasant thoughts.

Despite his distinctly upbeat frame of mind, Will found his mood shift as the road signs to the prison threatened that the gig venue was soon approaching. It was a deep and ingrained dark fear of institutions that rattled him, and was now understandably starting to get the better of him. The distinct uneasiness that he had tried to push away during the trip was now starting to creep up on him, and a slight clamminess on his hands with an all-too-familiar tightening of his stomach was beginning to make this whole venture seem like a terrible idea after all. The additional factor of being locked in took him back years to a place that he'd rather forget – unwelcome grim memories of the mental hospital that it would undoubtedly stir – making his heart beat louder and his breath shorten. One of his back teeth ached. He reminded himself that this was exactly one of those milestones that his psychiatrist had actively encouraged him to face head-on, and so he had bravely taken the bull by the horns when Dave first told him about this series of gigs, almost looking forward to the challenge. Now, though, that it had actually come about, he was clearly not enjoying the reality, but was determined to put his head down and get through it.

Peter Pilgrim mumbled to himself urgently and precisely, 'The healing and helping power of our Lord will guide and strengthen you. Don't fight your Destiny. We are all put on this Earth to help each other at different points in our lives, all stages in the Journey, and I know that I am here now for a reason – Jesus told me himself.' He was his own best friend, and seldom let anyone else in, so often found himself talking to himself. Peter noticed, as his thin lips trembled, that the carrots outside looked like they would soon need lifting, but maybe he'd give them another few days. As he surveyed this unremarkable morning, he noted again that the garden seemed fairly scrappy, expect the immaculate vegetable patch, which he tended regularly. This season's veggies were looking particularly healthy, which Peter attributed to his prayers for a bountiful crop and his yearly thanks and praise to God, especially around the time of Harvest Festival. Dark-leafed cabbages nestled alongside waywardly springing leeks, as parsnips, carrots and potatoes sensibly bordered the tidy and weed-free plot. He had always lived here, having been born and raised in this unexceptional house, which was his late parent's bungalow. Located on the outskirts of Aldershot, they had named it RonJoyce, and after they had both died Peter couldn't bring himself to change the name. It was the name of this little piece of England and should never be altered, that's just how it is. Not so much as a sniff of the concept of good taste had ever crossed the butterfly-design garden gate, and Ron Pilgrim's pebble-dash effect on the façade – lovingly added some twenty years ago – was now crumbling miserably, as was Joyce Pilgrim's yellow peeling wallpaper in the downstairs lavatory. He could almost see his dad, Ron, all dandruff and polished shoes, sat in his favourite chair with the newspaper, sometimes coughing or asking Joyce to bring him a cup of tea. Still, Peter loved the little house with all its faults – even the unidentifiable pungent aroma that for some mysterious reason always lingered in the tired kitchen, and his Father's words rang in his ears every time he stepped out of the olive-green front door to leave:

'Son, be good, and if you can't be good, be careful!'

Peter considered himself to be always good. In fact, he had made *being good* his entire lifetime's mission, devoting himself to God. This had become his raison d'être, especially over the last few years, and it had substantial and life-altering consequences. An insistence in spreading the Gospel relentlessly at any opportunity, particularly at work, had at first distanced but then scared off his fellow workers and finally his employers. Several warnings followed, at first gentle but gradually becoming more severe as his behaviour continued unchanging, and the inevitable eventually unfolded one bitterly cold February. It appeared that nearly ten years of duty at the pork pie factory counted for nothing, even after taking into account his almost religious zeal for the job at hand, coupled with a fanatical penchant for time-keeping. He felt like he'd been tossed out mercilessly with the waste after he was sacked, and the redundancy pay-out had been laughably derisory, a pittance that added insult to injury. Since the dismissal, Peter had picked up casual odd bits of gardening work, normally just about enough to support his fairly frugal existence. He enjoyed sitting around with a Cup-a-Soup (always the Minestrone with croutons), too much TV and playing chess against the computer. Not going out much, and not having friends as such, he spent a lot of his time with his dog Elvis, his only real companion. Elvis would sleep in Peter's bed, share the sofa with him, and made RonJoyce smell like a commercial boarding kennels complex on a hot day that was in urgent need of a hose-down. If Peter noticed, he certainly didn't let it bother him, and there was no one else around to complain. Once Elvis had nearly died, and Peter really had a fright. They never figured out what had caused the dog's intense sickness, which finally lifted after a week. Late one Friday night, a group of pissed-up lads were on their way home after an evening of boozing when one of them hurled up over the fence into the corner of RonJoyce's garden. Elvis greedily gobbled up the cold vomit early on Saturday morning when Peter let him out, before being stricken with a debilitating sickness that left him shaking for days, at 'death's door' according to Mr Halford the local vet. Peter would have been distraught if . . .

Yes, Peter was a loner and a misfit, and being a little bit odd was one of the things that he did best. He was the kind of guy who would get short-changed and not notice, or piss on his light-coloured slacks before walking out into a crowded room with dark marks down his leg. He couldn't even light a fire lighter, let alone start a fire. Groups of girls would whisper to each other before bursting into laughter around him. Once, at the annual Christmas work outing – this particular year at a Chinese restaurant – Peter had innocently drunk the dainty bowl of citrus-infused water that had come to the table for rinsing hands.

'Aaaahhhh,' he sighed, satiated, his workmates looking on, incredulous. 'That was delicious . . . nice and lemony.' He became, even more so, the object of ridicule back at the factory, which only accentuated his sense of isolation. When it came to factory tea breaks, he would cringe as someone would nearly always loudly ask him,

'Hey, Peter. How about a nice cup of hot lemon?'

Peter had endured a similar shameful humiliation when, years before, he had attended the funeral of a distant cousin in Cornwall. He had decided to book into a B&B for the night as the wake was due to last into the evening, so he planned to enjoy a much-needed mini-break from the pork pie factory. After being ushered into the breakfast room the following morning by the obsequious proprietor, he found a place with several fellow guests at a large table.

'And how would you like your eggs, sir?' he was asked.

Peter replied, to the ill-hidden amusement of many, 'Well done, please.' He had been too embarrassed to ever tell anybody this tale, and his egg intake since (poached, fried, scrambled or boiled) lowered considerably after this.

Rudely the phone would periodically shatter the usual peace and quiet of the bungalow, nearly always either someone attempting to sell something undoubtedly useless, or a mumbled apology for a wrong number. Peter sometimes wondered why he bothered paying for a phone line when these were the only calls he received. He never felt completely normal in himself when ambling around the town, especially on seeing carefree couples or laughing families out and about, apparently enjoying themselves. While desperately trying to fit in socially somewhere, he had at one stage attempted to hang out in a couple of local pubs, even drinking, but that had backfired. He was soon to discover that he would generally find himself ignored by most except perhaps the most hardened drinkers propping up the bar, who were intrigued by this strange and uncomfortable new arrival invading their space. Sometimes he might find himself sitting awkwardly at a table with a few people, but made a fool of himself in most cases. Like the time he managed to bore a young couple with details of his extensive teapot collection, a hobby and a passion that he had inherited from his beloved Uncle Eric.

The Albion had unfortunately long passed its glory days as a classic drinking haunt with an inviting rustic and womb-like feel, and as far as the décor was concerned, crimes against decency had sadly been committed in the name of modernity. The most unacceptable sacrilege had been the ruthless scrapping of the 18th century oak bar in order to install a clean and straight trendy bar *area*. The name had been changed to The Lion & Lobster, after 200 years or so as The Albion. A misjudged and overly-bright lighting design combined with a shoddily cheap refit gave the formerly welcoming Public House the feel of a second-rate furniture showroom. The atmosphere was that of a public library rather than a pub . . . not even an exciting library, some of which are known to fizzle with sexual tension! Obligatory sensible fire-exit signs screamed uncomfortably from every wall. There was not a pork scratching (with or without hairs still attached) or pie in sight, as the standard fare of yesteryear had been relegated to history. Interesting and unusual old-fashioned ales from niche British breweries had made way for garishly lit-up pumps of EU-manufactured chemical-rich lagers, and ashtrays now made way for bowls of olives, posh crisps or Japanese snacks. The pub had suffered an attack of *affluenza*, and now attempted to scrape some profit from its menu, serving pretentious offerings such as *Pan-seared Partridge with a Prune Jus, served on a bed of Seasonal Greens*, or *Line-Fished Pacific Halibut, Lentils, Scallions, and Sun-Dried Tomatoes, with a Lemon Feta Vinaigrette*. The bar staff were impossibly young and - while attempting desperately to be hip - apparently fresh from some kind of cheap fashion TV makeover. All this in Aldershot, of all places!

Outside an altercation was building momentum. A baseball-cap-wearing gentleman in a shiny tracksuit was wildly gesticulating in the face of an XXXL greasy lady with his packet of Mayfair cigarettes, while loudly establishing the fact that she was a 'fackin' caaaaaaannnnt!' Her much repeated response, delivered relentlessly at an even more elevated decibel level, was that the gentleman was also a 'fackin' caaaaaaannnnt,' who apparently also had 'got a fackin' problem.' As their discussion evolved slightly, their ugly muzzled dog wagged its ugly tail, before shitting on the middle of the pavement.

Inside, Peter was on a roll again with his teapot explanations, this time to four Aussie girls. At the table next to him, a gaggle of young friends were passing the evening taking turns showing each other 'funny' clips on YouTube. They would crane their necks to see a parakeet bobbing oddly on its perch, a chicken pecking on a keyboard or a dog playing with a kitten. This was all apparently hilarious, but these guys were in their 20s, not 15 or 16. It's good to have a laugh, but a bit sad that the Art of Conversation appears defunct, Peter thought. The second pint of Becks Vier (clever . . . *eins, zwei, drei, vier*% alcohol) had gone straight to Peter's head, and he was unusually animated.

'You wouldn't believe my Yixing pot, it's just incredible

. . . the colouring and craftsmanship are second to none. What you have to appreciate about each and every teapot that you acquire is its individual and specific quality, down to the efficiency of the actual pour itself, or the feel of it when you lift it up by the handle. It's weight, glaze, and general look are all important factors, you know. Of course, I haven't even mentioned the rarity factor . . . how many were originally produced? How many are surviving in good condition, etc?'

He didn't pause, in fact he gathered pace and his voice rose and gained slightly in volume as his excitement grew. 'Where does it come from, this beautiful specimen? You look for the maker's mark, you see, but they don't always have one so sometimes you have to be a bit of a teapot Hercule Poirot! Or in your case, ladies, more like a young Miss Marple, I suppose!' He snorted involuntarily as he chortled at this quip, even though the girls hadn't a clue what he was talking about. His irritating habit of nervously tapping his right foot at speed was operating to its maximum, his white thigh mercifully covered by its nasty trousers vibrating up and down like a piston.

'They are all deliciously unique and have their own quirks, you know. You'll get some that might be absolute turkeys to pour but make up for it in their special styling . . .' He waffled on, even suddenly springing up to the bar at one point to seek out pen and paper, before eagerly noting down teapot aficionado reference book titles and website addresses for the girls.

'Hey, you've got to check out his shoes, guys.' (She meant *girls* but these Aussie girls generally called each other *guys*). 'Don't they look like those weird Cornish pasty things the Brits eat, but stuck on his feet – have you seen them?'

The girls tittered as the Cornish pasties and their owner

motored eagerly back to the table. They had no idea that they'd actually got off lightly thus far as he hadn't even started digressing about his fascination with vintage ice-cream vehicles. 'That guy has *got* to be a virgin,' one of the bemused girls commented on their giggly stumble home later that night. 'Paralysingly dull!' added another. Neither one was wrong.

Peter was also somewhat on an expert on what he would label as jazz, but what is really cheesy, light jazz-soul. The girls were lucky on this occasion to have been spared his enthusiastic ramblings about his favourite groups: Spyro Gyra, David Sanborn or The Yellowjackets. He couldn't grasp Charlie Parker, yet his eyes would well up listening to Kenny G's moving melodies. John Scofield would give him a headache, but Lee Ritenour's joyous tunefulness would restore a smile. He occasionally went to these types of concerts, and would avidly take notes throughout with a little well-sharpened pencil and his notebook. This is another topic the girls were fortunate to miss on this particular night: *the importance of a fine pencil.*

He may well have explained, if given the chance. . .

'It's the accuracy of the glide, the sheer beauty of the wood, combined with natural contact with quality paper. While others may look contemptuously as they play around with their smartphones, it feels great to be writing as everyone taps idiotically at their awkward tiny screens. This is also where an expensive notebook comes into play – it always gives one the impression that one is writing something important.'

Another similarly calamitous incident was the time that a predatory middle-aged and recently divorced woman decided that that she had found her prey for the evening, and she certainly knew what she wanted. Having found out that her mendacious husband had been having his way with someone at work, she had divorced him almost immediately and received a hefty settlement agreed upon through their expensive lawyers. The fact that it had been his secretary seemed so pathetic to her, what a cliché! Had the man she had married so long ago no more imagination? She had been *enjoying* herself this evening, celebrating her pay-out alone with a bottle or two of the pub's very mediocre white wine, and was rapidly becoming dangerously wobbly on her unsuitably tarty high heels. Peter was genuinely scared stiff with this undesired and certainly unlikely attention, and he scarcely knew what to say as she perched herself down opposite him at his small table. After listening to her slurred tale of failed marriage and costly separation, with its new tale of a successful pay-out, Peter bought himself another pint to steady his nerves. She was ranting when he arrived back at the table, 'And you see, dear, I always seem to attract the absolute bastards, wankers the lot of them. It must be a special skill I have, magnet for the rotten male, it's part of my character. I'm not gonna candy-coat it, he's an absolute dick. Look at this I just sent him, this'll fuck him up.' She held up her mobile phone, displaying a simple message: *Love u xxxx.*

Her spiteful cackle jumped out at him, followed by a brief flash of ugly smile. Peter was getting in a pickle. 'It doesn't seem fair, really, when it happens again and again. That's why I'm hitting the Lady Petrol tonight.' There was a momentary pause as she concentrated to pour herself a huge glass of wine, getting most of it in the glass. 'It's always about men. They always end up showing their true colours. That's why these days I'm just after a good time when I can get it, if you know what I mean . . . I mean, fuck it, fifteen years of emotional and financial stress with very little sex in return . . .' she bleated on, embittered in her rambling. Starting to sweat, he sat back down, which was the cue for the drunken women to start whispering over the table to him, sweaty bosom heaving and straining, suggesting things that Peter had never heard of before and certainly never tried. A confused and all-consuming concoction of alcohol, sexual arousal, ignorance and complete bloody panic swiftly seized him up and overtook his entire body and mind. He ran all the way home without stopping or even turning around after giving her the slip on the pretence of 'going to inspect the plumbing – it must be all the beer.' The only person he remembered seeing on the way back was a grossly overweight woman all alone in the Chinese all-you-can-eat-buffet-for-£4.95, opposite STARBURGER (where a gut-busting Dirty Burger will only set you back £3.95). She was so wide that she looked like she would fill a sofa in the way most mortals fill an armchair, and would probably rest stubby arms on the arm rests on either side. She was sporting a T-shirt proudly proclaiming *I'm 99% Perfect*. Peter was never to know how she had recently enjoyed a massive boost to her confidence since the removal of an unsightly wart on her upper left cheek, but he did notice how her outsized stomach appeared to start at her neck. Glancing up at him guiltily over her plastic tray, she discarded her binge-induced shame into the bin, along with a few grains of rice and sucked prawn tails that her chubby hands scraped off her plate, before her lonely waddle home past the horse hospital then right to the end of the road and up to her tiny flat above the sexual health clinic with the pale green logo.

Some graffiti on the side of some flats looked fresh, he'd not noticed it before . . .

If you don't wanna die
←*walk*
←*calm*

He didn't understand it – all he knew is that he was running and he certainly wasn't calm. Was it meant for him personally? This troubled him deeply, emphasizing his panic and engulfing him with an intensely disturbing paranoia that was so strong it eclipsed any feeling he had ever experienced.

Knees weak with fear and in a cold sweat, he found himself trembling as he fumbled with the lock. The evening had been weird. Once back inside the familiar and warm safety of RonJoyce, he prayed to God for forgiveness as he cowered alone on the sofa with a lump in his throat, heart pounding against his skinny frame. He tore off his new Primark black, smart, going-out trousers that he had inadvertently pissed in slightly and went to put them in the washing machine, a silver Beko CY560 1200 spin, noticing at this point that he had gone out with loads of Elvis' dog hairs down the left trouser leg. The label, he noticed, said *DRY CLEAN ONLY*. 'At £8 it'd be cheaper to buy a new pair every time!' he said out loud as he bundled them into the machine anyway. This was the point at which he gave up on the pub project, and indeed any other form of interaction out in the world in general. The language and filthy discussion that went on in such establishments upset him, and the experiment had run its course. He just wasn't cut out for normal life, he decided. This was – without him realising it at the time – an important turning point in his Journey, it being the point at which his religious ardour suddenly stepped up a gear or two, dangerously altering from playing a significant part of his life to now becoming his obsession.

The dark prison gates eventually swung open unceremoniously, groaning under their own weight, following a lengthy exchange at the main security post. How many nervous and unwilling men had met their fate and followed this same path into the building, and listened with dread to that same ominous sound? Orange and white lights ahead enticed the van to gingerly creep into the building, and the unwelcome engulfing feeling of being trapped in an institution fell over them all. No-one in the band had ever set foot in a prison before and they didn't really know what to expect. It was a lot less high-tech than Will had imagined, and seemed fairly straightforward and basic – tall walls, fences, a few windows, and grim buildings constantly being monitored by CCTV. A stark scene, certainly an odd venue for a gig. Will felt surprisingly calm upon entering the compound, and he thought that perhaps his shrink was right: he must attack and face any fears head-on. There then followed a routine that they would all soon become accustomed to after a few more prison gigs. Three wardens took them into a bright holding area with an exceptionally shiny floor where they were rigidly explained the search procedure. They were all to be patted down, sniffed by a drugs dog whether they liked it or not, followed by a walk through a scanner. Meanwhile, the van was undergoing a thorough inspection, as was the gear, which had all been unloaded. The wardens appeared especially ordinary to Will, who for reasons only known to himself was expecting some burly aggressive types. He felt quite silly that he'd even entertained such idiotic preconceptions, so changed his train of thought to question how the cleaners could have managed such an impressive lustre from the floor. There was a fair amount of hanging around, and Will pondered his life. He knew that it couldn't be the guitar for ever, and that he'd have to try something else – perhaps his other passion, photography. Coffee-table photographic books enthralled him, and he had a few ideas up his sleeve for titles of his own: Washing Lines from around the Globe, The History of Buttons, Cheese Lover's Selection: Vol I, Roundabouts of France, and Male Dwarves and their Wives: a Portrait, (with the potential for a follow-up: Female Dwarves and their Husbands: a Portrait). He'd have to have a more serious think about this, he decided. As for the gig, the drummer's snare was tinny and tuned far too high, the bass player's low E-string was audibly sharp, and the keyboard player's amp was too loud, forcing everyone to endure bright polybrass patches and terrible Hammond B-3 emulations. Medleys should be illegal, and Bob Marley should never be covered. A few hours later – late that afternoon – as he indifferently replicated the funk guitar grooves on 'Ain't no Stoppin' us Now' and three hundred lucky inmates bobbed their heads to the band in the terrible acoustics of the gymnasium, Will considered that he'd achieved the zenith of the strangest moment of his life so far . . . and he'd certainly had some odd ones.

Peter sliced his hand open viciously as razor-sharp metal slipped suddenly and flew upwards. He hadn't been concentrating on the task, his mind wandering as it had been uncommonly preoccupied lately. Thick fishy oil and sardine pieces scattered across the kitchen floor, their oblong tin coffin skidding quickly over the linoleum, only coming to a halt as it bashed into the skirting board. He wished that he'd gone for the figs with bread option instead (he's had a long-standing love/hate relationship with figs), but today he wasn't interested in the little slimy fruits. Now thin luminous blood gushed generously from the fresh deep gash, cascading off the tips of his fingers and dripping down dramatically, spattering the floor. Serenely he waited at the sink for the bleeding to abate, before calmly clearing up the stinking mess, deliberately and meticulously wiping and cleaning until all traces of fish and blood had gone. Only after this task had been dealt with did he turn attention to himself. For the next ten minutes he busied himself with bandages, creams and pain. Then he reached up to open a cupboard and pulled out another identical tin of sardines from the neatly stacked arrangement, but this time – as he had done so many times before – he managed to successfully fork its contents onto a few of his favourite dry biscuits without further injury. A Simpsons mug full of strong instant coffee sat steaming on the sideboard, as – despite his teapot collection – Peter was a regular coffee drinker. He weakly tugged open the fridge to search for the milk that he was sure wasn't there, only to be confronted with the bleak scene so well known to many – the Bachelor Fridge, full with space. Butter-replacement spread (only a few scrapes left), some tragic dregs lining a ketchup bottle, mysterious and ancient chutney items, an old humble onion (a most underrated vegetable), and was that mustard at the back, there? No milk. Glancing up, a lonely shelf offered just the one tin of baked beans, an untouched bottle of Irish whisky nestling behind it apologetically. Peter was missing a housewife, he often thought to himself, or were they called housemakers these days? Trundling through to the living room with his modest snack, his nerves jangled, his thoughts in constant turmoil, and he felt shaky and unsettled. A brain fog swept over his troubled mind as he slouched into the familiar sofa. Why was the bombing, occupying, torturing, killing and maiming with drones carried out by the Christians around the world eating away at him so much? For the last few weeks now he had sat for hours on end at RonJoyce with the TV telling tales of horror from faraway lands, and he had not been able to sleep properly. CNN, Sky News, BBC . . . he dived between them all, even often enduring long worldwide weather broadcasts, mainly as he'd grown to love the smooth jazz guitar bedding music that accompanied them. He spent most of his time carrying out his new research, as a plethora of constantly accessible media information had just been opened up to him by way of his recent internet connection at the bungalow. Sensing that the floodgates had kindly been opened for him from a Higher Place, he would either learn through his internet findings or intensely pray, finding an unknown joy in both activities never before experienced to such an acute degree. While feeding avidly off the TV every day and surfing websites all day and much of the night, Peter's renaissance was unfolding at an alarming rate, without any deliberate effort on his part. It seemed that he had suddenly found something deep down that he had unwittingly been searching for all this time over many years, and he now felt that he didn't have a second to waste. He had created an air of expectation around himself – for himself – and he felt enormously energised and invigorated. Now sitting down in the musty living room with his modest fishy snack, he stared at the screen, he stared at the pretty blonde newsreader who had just followed on from Plasticman the Anchorman. Now, was she a journalist or an actress? Whatever her personal career history, she was unexpectedly cut off – a violent juxtaposition of intense war scenes and images of despair and devastation filling her place. The pensive man sipped at his scolding hot cheap coffee. His appetite abruptly deadened, he pressed the bandaged hand until it smarted angrily, then he pressed some more, now rubbing it aggressively until acrid tears of agony were pulling themselves down his face, blood freshly leaking and dripping onto the floor. He continued to watch as the images blurred through his tears, the pain giving him a pronounced kick of satisfaction. This somehow made him feel purer following the TV's spilt poison spewing into the room and dirtying him. His mood lifted, the tears stopped.

Anger and distress seemed to have been thrust upon his shoulders for a reason: his former eccentric characteristics now morphed towards a driven dedication and perspective that concentrated into an intense Higher Purpose that Peter intended to fulfil. He developed an addiction to watching video clips of clerics online and resolved to cultivate a beard. His recent self-appointed place deep within terrorist websites and the internet chatrooms of cyberspace had provided him with an long-overdue and warm sense of belonging, particularly after having been marginalised in the town and beyond. A craving for acceptance was satisfied at long last. *What love he had once held in his heart for his Christian God!* All the guilt that had welled up inside him joined with his pent-up frustration and fuelled his fascination with the aura surrounding Jihad. His new-found adoration of Islamist Fundamentalism – even Islamofachism – was nearing completion, with the switch in his brain most certainly in the ON position. It satisfied his craving for a purpose in life, and he became certain of having found his own meaning of existence, however unaware of the nefarious thought processes that were involuntarily unfolding.

When he pictured the future, he felt only clarity and joy in his mind, heart and soul. The Christians were the Infidels, evil warriors sent by the Devil. Decadent Britain – this filthy toilet – must, and will, be held to account. These people have to be punished, they shall be made to pay, *they must be punished* . . .

Ron and Joyce Pilgrim had been gentle folk. Life was a simple yet rewarding adventure for them, and the birth of their one and only child was nothing other than a miracle in their eyes. It had been said repeatedly by the doctors that it would never happen, and after more than ten years of otherwise happy marriage both of them had reluctantly resigned themselves to the fact that they would be a childless couple. Baby Peter arrived unexpectedly just short of two months early, and although he was a delicate little boy, mother and baby were doing well and enjoyed being comfortably back home at RonJoyce within the week. An unremarkably conventional upbringing followed, peppered liberally with religion. This would be administered both at school and in the home, and Sundays meant a trip to church, without fail. It was here that an early talent was discovered and subsequently nurtured, as Peter's strong and distinctive singing voice during congregational hymn-singing had not gone unnoticed by Mr. Hicks the choirmaster. The elderly Mr. Hicks ran an eager and welcoming modest choir, with Peter being the sole child. Some might unkindly point out that in the case of many of the singers their enthusiasm perhaps outweighed their talent, nevertheless for Peter it felt marvellous to be a part of it, and the choir did undoubtedly have sporadic special moments. He also found it blissfully enchanting being among this group of worshippers, who were obsessed by such funny robes, nose-curling incense and perplexingly bizarre rituals. *Why do these grown men wander about so deliberately with candles, kneeling and bowing at times with such devout reverence? What is the reason for these meandering, monotone sermons and never-ending prayers? These muttered monologues and strange murmurings, what's it all about?* It was simply how it was in church, he surmised. Despite these ongoing perplexities, he considered the singing part to be great fun and learnt to appreciate both the delicate grace and purity of Plainsong, as well as enjoying the complex and intricate harmonies and soaring melodies that occurred in much of Mr. Hicks' other chosen repertoire. The constant encouragement that Mr. Hicks selflessly provided proved invaluable, and it was the advice of the choirmaster to Ron and Joyce that was to determine the next important stage of young Peter's life. Over cups of hot, sweet, instant coffee in the 1960s-built church hall after one especially drawn-out service, Mr. Hicks strongly recommended to the proud parents that they should make contact with some of the top London choir schools with the view to presenting Peter at the upcoming auditions for their cathedral choirs. 'You see,' he explained deliberately, 'the boy has a certain talent which it would be a great shame to waste or let go by the wayside. There are opportunities for boys like him, doors to open at such an early age, a start in life that others could only dream of, and experiences the value of which money can never buy. These age-old establishments offer a wealth of experience and tradition that Pilgrim Junior could embrace, including a top-notch education that would all be part of the package when he passes the necessary audition, of course. It's an entire world that Peter would soak up, and it would affect the rest of his life.' Mr. Hicks wouldn't live long enough to discover quite how true his words were, but for now Ron and Joyce were rapt, hanging on every word that the choirmaster carefully chose. He had unwittingly assumed almost a salesman's role, the simple and proud parents – his clients – on the cusp of purchasing a timeshare in a war zone, or an over-priced off-plan apartment in a collapsing economy that would never be built. Mr. Hicks offered to write a glowing letter of reference for the lad, intending to pack it full of superlatives, for he only had praise to offer. Ron and Joyce took all that Mr. Hicks had to say on board, before politely making their excuses to leave. All that singing, standing, kneeling, thinking, listening and praying in a cold church would make anyone work up an appetite, and they had only nibbled on one miserable biscuit since the service. The biscuit box lid hadn't been closed properly by one of the church hall spinsters the previous Sunday, and disastrously the party selection had gone horribly stale. Peter had tried a second biscuit, but on finding it just as hideously unpalatable as the first he scanned the area to ensure he wasn't being watched before secreting it surreptitiously down the back of one of the hall radiators into the waiting pillow of dust and hair.

A while later, back at RonJoyce, Ron and Joyce discussed the choirmaster's suggestion excitedly with their son over their late Sunday lunch, roast lamb this week, which couldn't have arrived soon enough for Peter. *Meat.* The carefree, innocent boy was happily going along with their plan, although he would have no idea of what it would entail in reality, as of course he knew little of the world at his age. In any case, his immediate attention was being held by the dilemma concerning him: what combination of meat and vegetables he could load onto his fork, which right now was far more important.

Six months later, young Peter's cold nose was pressed up

against the window at the front of the top deck of a London Routemaster bus. His breath left a natural canvas on the grubby glass so he quickly scribbled pictures with his finger before they would magically disappear. The tinkling stopping bell of the bus every couple of minutes made him laugh, and the sheer number of passengers rushing onto or jumping off the big red tin was amazing. The way that such intense energy could be somehow packed into and contained in such a densely-filled place made a great and lasting impression on him. That, along with the sheer business of life, as people scurried about clutching important-looking bags and fresh newspapers, or vanished down dark stairwells and through fast-revolving doors. People looked so different here, and the apparent randomness of their actions confused him: how could everyone here have a specific purpose and play their own part in oiling this machine that was such a manic metropolis? This new frenzied world that was the crazy city delighted and entranced him immediately, having never seen so much activity, or such majesty and beauty in the surrounding buildings. Why was his home town not be more like this . . . couldn't the *powers that be* make Aldershot carry out some more construction work and become a thriving new power to rival London? His decision was made in a flash: this was where he wanted to be from now on.

A slightly sterile audition early that afternoon felt to Peter as if it was over before it had even started, but what had escaped him completely was the fact that he had breezed through it effortlessly and was soon to be on his way to becoming a chorister in one of the elite top cathedral choirs in the world.

Norman took acid. He started to feel weird after 15 miNutes or so. He was fully weird after 30 minutes. DrippINg taps, they seemed to be everywhere, even coming oUt of his scratched wristwatch. The existence of so mANY diffERent varietieS of pasta is suddenly fascinating: shells, tUBEs, tiny oNes or endless sheets of lasagna pasta,CURly, long and short, strAIght and curly pieces in all shades of colours, dryy oR fressssbh.

1011100100100110100100001110100101100101000011010010100111110000. What's that UNKnown laNguage that he keeps heARing, and who'S the strange girl with the electRIc blue hair in pigtails, and is she attraCtive? I want 2 Go MIdgEt-kiCking iN PRaGue, or pErhaps wE should aLL gO to The muSeum of MoUld. The corners of the room MELt and curve, all abrupt lines soften and bend. The room turns into an Italian chapel, with freScos painted on the ceiling. Suddenly, Is that GAs ? Perhaps Yatter has left the oven on. norman fiNDs an unopened pIZZa looking lonely sitting in a cold oven, so he takes it out carefully, puts it on the forMICa kitchen table, and splurts ketchUp all over the plastic packaging. My God, tell me I'm nOt in a Yorkshire forced-rhubaRb farm, please. Can U GeT freeze-DrieD water? (jUst add wHat?!!) hoW aBout chiLLi watEr? 100 0110 010101000100001111110. ThE nEw aulD Queen album pLAys in the living room, and Norman cAn quite clearly hear galloping horses throughout the track 'Radio GAGA.' How do they record THAt? Maybe Freddie was sending a signal with those initials GA – Groove Armada? Was Freddie actUAlly the UK inventor of LonDOn dance musIC, or some kind of Godfather figUre? Has ScoTt been to SCOtlaNd? His watch Gets louder, so he checks it and he disappears through the face, rushes through tHe mechanism dodging spokes and wheels wIth dangerous-looking spikes, suddenly *ending up in a bright children's TV progrAmme, where the gIrl with the German-style pigtails is smiling at him. She looks liKe his sister Polly. Should he go to Munich, maybe to open a school or a Nazi woOd-choPping centre? Customers could pay handsomely to dress up as superMan to cut logs with an axe, then to be served with bratWurst and lashing of fine bEer, and given a 'free' copy of Mein Kampf upon their departure. Wow, the business ventures Norman can conjure from nowhere! BuT being a page turner for CoNcert piaNists has Got 2 B a gReaaaT jOb . . . buT tHen thEre's a DOUbt whether oR noT they Use sHeet Music on StAge?* 10000100101111111. *I NeeD my BaY SicK hu Mann wriTES, lyke be ING abeL 2 maykE a KuP ov T. Dust everywhere – in his eyes, lungs, nose, ears, he is being engulfed and feels as if he is under attack. This is not going so well. SuD en LEE, iS tHAt a PLaIcE? Music off. Must do something to occupy the brain matter.* 1000101101111111100. *go back into the kitchen and make some sandwiches for Yatter for the morning: white sliced bread with rAw bacon. This takes nearly an hour. Norman has a waking dream about being part of a multi-coloured strangely pixilated soap opera.*

Peter sits on the couch at Ronjoyce and writes back to his new friends, the militant cyberspace contacts in SE Asia, tapping away noisily on his computer keyboard, sentences seeming to fly onto the screen from the tips of his fingers, a hideous vein bulging on the side of his damp forehead, nerves and senses on full alert and his brain buzzing with excitement:

They will not be permitted to crush this movement by repression, and we will ensure that the grotesque inequalities will be ironed out. The Great Revolution has already commenced, the Establishment already acknowledges us as a serious threat, and so they should! An internal Jihad of the heart and soul is not adequate, so we must impress upon our fellow people the necessity of Jihad by the sword. They can hunt us like mad dogs, but I can blend in seamlessly with my people, and I know that we must meet their violence with our own violence, which must be three hundred times more destructive than their feeble attempts to destroy us. Does their humanity matter? I say 'NO' and I am certain that the corpses of our enemies will smell sweet. Their disgusting ways and sins must not be tolerated, the drinking, drug-taking, devil-like music, blatant baring of flesh offensively . . . such Munkar will be punished. I am desperate to help, and I will make this my life's goal until I achieve it or die trying. Allah has written out everything, it is all prepared and in His hands. The acts of the assassin will most certainly be rewarded copiously in heaven, and you must pray for me that I will be martyred in a state of pure faith. My mission will be the ultimate one-way ticket, and I will be proud to fulfil my Destiny in such a manner. I have found enlightenment and my radicalisation is complete. I fully submit to the One who has created us . . . I am yours.

He stops suddenly and stares ahead, tiny beads of sweat glistening on his forehead, left knee bouncing slightly as his heel taps unremittingly on the carpet. Elvis stirs on the couch, turns and studies him inquisitively. Even the dog senses something serious, as his master anticipates his forthcoming title: The White Islamist Bomber, and looks forward impatiently to finding a role for his mission. He was determined to finally count for something and to carve out his own specialist position in Britain's increasingly disturbing milieu of celebrity worship . . .

So what was it about this French farmer that magnetised Sue towards him so strongly? It certainly couldn't have been his dress sense – or lack of it – which appeared to be stuck in some medieval century, mixed up with a few hypermarket pieces tossed in randomly for good measure, along with the denim shirts. Nor must it be his looks, as he could never be described as a classically handsome man by any stretch of the imagination. Although he had about him a certain ruggedness and self-confidence that appealed to the ladies, it was perhaps the cheeky glint in his eye that Sue found more and more irresistible. His mellow temperament and her desire to venture into unknown territory also played a strong part in her decision to further the affair, but it was like a bolt out of the blue that Claude ignited yet another passion for Sue, that surprised even herself. Was it her reward to herself for hitting forty? Maybe so. He had prepared crêpes with citron et sucre for them in the middle of the afternoon one rainy day, and cheekily served them with a crisp and fruity dry white Saumur, perfectly chilled. The seduction was complete, and the charming Frenchman had her like putty in his hands. He also introduced her to a world of French chansons that she had previously dismissed out of hand. Tom's musical tastes didn't stretch further than Dire Straits, Eric Clapton or Coldplay – anything else he would pretty much scoff at, and Sue had lived with this for far too long. Claude opened up a whole new life for Sue in general, also unwittingly stirring in her this new-found passion for French pop music from the 1960s and 70s that made her feel unusually youthful and revitalised. As far as Claude was concerned, Sue was an angel sent from heaven. He recalled the first time he had laid his eyes on her: her paper-white complexion and delicate flat nose appearing almost glued onto her tiny face, proportional to her doll-like features. His English Rose. Whilst she could perhaps not traditionally be considered a beauty, there was something special in the way that she held herself and wore her clothes: appealing curves of her body created gentle ripples across her hippy-ish cream-lined linen blouse. Claude was mildly excited to glimpse a soft blond down just viewable on her upper breast. Crossing her legs high, in a vaguely supermodel-like pose, her manicured left hand casually slumped on her lap. He was convinced that she was the type of woman that other females secretly despised as they would be jealous of her looks and personality, and he concluded that men would fall at her feet. This was not actually the case, but it's certainly what Claude envisioned through the fog of his light-headed predestination. He would gaze at the soft nape of her neck, and wonder in awe at such delicious delicacy in the make-up of her chin and its perfect line up to her petal lips, her hair tucked behind an ear on one side, falling across her forehead enticingly on the other.

'Soft hands, firm breasts,' he sighed into her ear often when out in public, even in front of their respective spouses, causing her to titter – his comical accent for some reason heightening her excitement and arousal. His faithful but frumpy wife had absolutely no idea of his liaison with Sue until one otherwise perfectly normal day after lunch, Claude calmly let her know that he would be leaving her for the English lady. Taking into consideration the fact that they had been married for just short of thirty years, she stoically retained her composure, almost as if she could expect nothing less and it was just a matter of time until he would drop such a bombshell. She had, in reality, not suspected a thing regarding Claude's infidelity, his words now flowing almost straight past her, only to drift out of the open window and across the wide fields, blown away into the haze by friendly breezes. The words became fluffy and distant, muffled in their thick cloud of deceit yet somehow still sinking in all the same, lodging themselves somewhere in the deep recesses of her brain. 'I'll always love you, you do know that, don't you.' She remained blank. His rambling meant less and less, never hesitating or pausing, as if the more he uttered the less substantial the disappointment and heartache would be for her, diluted by explanation.

'I can smell sausages, oh that's gooood. This cloud is amazing because it feels so light but I'm not falling through, and is that . . . ? Is that . . . ? No, it can't be . . . yes, it bloody well is!

It's Rick Astley, and he's frying up sausages on MY cloud, doing the odd little boogie as he browns the sausages to perfection. His lips are moving and he may be singing, a brilliant sheen on his hair. I am aware that he's cooking for me'.

This strange yet comforting scene lasts for some time, although the perception of time doesn't exist. It could have been hours, and it felt right. As if mildly distracted and put off his stride, Rick stops singing for a second and fixes me squarely in the eye.

'Ah, you're here. Would you like mustard on your sausage?' he asks nonchalantly. 'That'd be lovely, Rick.' I hear my own steady voice reply, although distantly.

RA: 'But listen here my friend, and listen carefully. Only if you change your name from Peter to Ahmed will I grant your wish regarding the meat portion and its delicious side condiment of mustard. It will be a fine English mustard. You will be known as Ahmed from henceforth, then . . . and only then . . . will I furnish you with mustard on your sausage.'

Ahmed: 'Ok, Rick, okay. Anything you say. You're the boss on this cloud, I am merely a lucky tourist in your celestial kitchen.'

I want to talk some more but my throat is dry and I have nothing to say. Somehow the cloud floats off, fading away with Rick Astley still on it, still dancing beautifully, hips swinging, and lovingly turning sausages. He may even be singing again . . .

Peter woke up with a start, an unfeasibly strained erection pressing uncomfortably into his ill-fitting polyester trousers. He tried, but failed, to recall the last time that he had achieved wood. His good hand was nurturing it and all he could view in his mind's eye was a hot sausage liberally plastered with hot mustard. *Wow, this is weird,* he thought. He found himself still on the couch with the TV on, his wounded hand throbbing as well as his penis – but somehow none of that mattered. From this moment he was to call himself Ahmed, because he *knew* that the dream had been sent from above for a purpose, and *he* had been chosen. Rick Astley had confirmed this: it was as simple as that, black and white.

Peter, now Ahmed, leant over to where his laptop had been on overnight charge. On checking his email inbox, he found a long-anticipated message from his new mentor. It was the message finally and officially acknowledging his acceptance into the terrorist spectrum, but more importantly incorporating the go-ahead for Ahmed to become a fully active operative. It became crystal clear to Ahmed that the dream and the email could not have simultaneously occurred by coincidence. There were higher powers at work here, and as far as he was concerned, everything was coming together just as he wished. He scratched at his ever-bushier beard and trudged into the kitchen for a mug of coffee.

'So she just sat there, almost dream-like, melancholic but I think understanding, and listened to my words, you see? I tried to break it gently, but there's no easy way of course.' Claude gulped his Pastis, the ice cubes rattling resonantly in Sue Ellen from Dallas style. Odd drops of rain pattered sparsely on the tall, thin windows.

'I think that what is going to happen, you know, I think she will be going to move in with her sister in town. She has a spare room and I am certain that it's to be for the best. It will take some time to organise, but then you can come to live with me here. It feels like a lot of positivity shrouded in negativity. I told her that I love you now, and that . . . well, I thanked her I suppose, in a way, *oui*, I *thanked her* for all our years together and . . .' Claude tailed off, running out of steam and bowing his head. It had been an emotionally exhausting afternoon, and he was unloading it all onto Sue now.

'Listen, darling, I'm proud of you,' she applauded him. 'We just have to sort out the mechanics of the thing but, you know, the worst is over. She'll get used to the idea given time, and now it's all down to me. Tom's going to be much harder to tell . . . you'll probably see me with a black eye later!'

She was only half-joking.

'If he even comes close to raising a hand you run straight back to me, okay? Ok?' Claude reddened somewhat.

'Don't worry yourself, Claude, I'll be fine. Now listen, I'd better head home and get this over and done with. You know, the sooner the better and all that. Wish me luck.'

'*Bon courage, chéri.*' Claude kissed her deeply, before holding her tight, enjoying the sensation of her warm breath on his neck. 'We will see each other in a little while.' He was hoping that she would carry out her mission with clear eyes and a cold heart, and would be ready to dedicate her life to him alone from now on.

Sue bounded over the threshold into the farm courtyard, the rain now tumbling from the heavens in diagonal sheets, momentarily stunning her. 'What's going on with this shit?' she cursed to herself. It really was the kind of weather that only a cow or chicken could tolerate. Jumping into the driver's seat, she sank back and checked her make-up in the rear-view mirror. 'I think that I need to iron my face,' she told her imaginary passenger. The image that stared back at her was a middle-aged woman whom she failed to recognise, cold eyes and wet cheeks, as if she'd been crying. She was aware that her decision and forthcoming actions would be monumental in her life, and while brushing off the rain and freshening up her lipstick she mentally strengthened herself for the break-up with her husband that she was about to initiate. The decision she had made weeks previously, but the definite action she had scheduled for this very day, and the day had come along sooner than imagined.

'Here goes,' she mumbled to herself, turning the ignition. Abruptly flushed with optimism, she added out loud: 'tank's full of juice, let's roll!' As she pulled away, Sue considered Tom's recent 'joke' about her choice of car, what *exactly* had he said? It came back to her: 'Ah, you bought an automatic. Interesting choice. Well, too bad, they're just for women and amputees really.' Remembering this gave her a boost as it convinced her that she was doing the right thing leaving this man, whose humour and demeanour had over the years become more and more damning, cruel, sexist and distasteful. A look of intense concentration descended over her determined face as she slowly negotiated the car around and started off down the track towards her marital home.

Meanwhile, back in London, Yatter was compiling his book of poetry, titled *The Bad Poet's Society.* He had a new entry, one of his favourites, that had come to him in a flash of inspiration, just like that!

RULE NUMBER ONE

Don't trust 'normal' people
Don't believe 'normal' people
Don't trust 'normal' people
Don't believe 'normal' people.

By Yatter

Young Peter never understood exactly what went on in the teacher's apartments that adjoined the dormitories. The two live-in teachers whose job it was also to administer care at the bijou choir school – a mere 38 pupils – both had favourites who would be selected to watch TV after lights-out. The dark goings-on behind these doors finally led to the downfall of both the monsters. These deviants were not to get their comeuppance until some thirty years later, in separate historic abuse trials initiated by six former students and investigated by CID's Historical Child Abuse Unit. However, the men both received laughably light sentences for their paedophilia and acts of abuse; for some unknown reason only a few years of prison each. Peter remembered certain things – the acrid smell of vinegar, used to steep canes in order to smarten the sting – but . . .

Many years later as a young man, Peter tried to come to terms with the abuse that he had suffered, but he could not process the information, the reasoning, the suffering. The sexual abuse triggered and subsequently nourished his disjointed view of life, fragments of reality distorted through cloudy water. On top of the tampering, it was the relentless indoctrination into the Christian faith – daily cathedral services and additional ones on weekends, that also helped to push him to the edge of reason, confusing and confounding him. He had a strange memory that one of the visiting Latin teachers had been 'allowed to leave' after being arrested in a supermarket for shoplifting a chicken, dressed as a woman. They'd caught that one at the time, but not the kiddie-fiddlers. A total failure of trust in authority and order in life ensued, and a general meltdown deep in Peter's brain and emotional capacity manifested itself fully into adulthood. It was not until his 20s that Peter turned back to God and became *Born Again*. He finally became comfortable in himself and was generally in a soft state of religious elation, enjoying gardening, long shifts at the pork pie factory, and his trusty dog Elvis, for several years. Unfortunately this could not last as life turned sour with war, and more war, and endless suffering, and it was only when he arrived at this crossroads of violence that Peter searched for and found an alternative path: *Ahmed the Operative.*

Somewhere around the nondescript outskirts of Cheltenham, supercomputers whirred around the clock in the doughnut-shaped building that called itself GCHQ. The 5,500-strong team of employees at Government Communications Headquarters had their work cut out for them, but for the majority it was a dream posting – serving their country and working for the greater good while carrying out interesting and well-paid work in their chosen field. Linguists, mathematicians, codebreakers, analysts, technology buffs, computer nerds and intelligence experts made up some of the collective brain power gathered together in this place – lots of glasses and beards, along with millions of pounds worth of equipment and highly-powered gear designed to combat terrorism and any similar threat. GCHQ's role included eavesdropping on global communications, such as ISIS radio traffic, a telling email or text traffic. Even though Ahmed had been digging deeply online, he was nowhere on either the police or Special Service's radars, and it was highly likely that things would remain like this. Despite the extensive resources available to the Government through the echelons of power within various departments, Ahmed was what's known as a *clean skin*. In other words, he had no criminal record, was not an Arab, and generally did not fit in with the perceived profile of a deadly and ruthless bomber. This was to work hugely to his advantage, his apparently humdrum existence arousing no suspicion at all around the streets of Aldershot or further afield. All the while, this strange little man was planning and plotting, scheming and arranging, looking forward to his big moment that was approaching sooner all the time . . .

'How d'you spell *Caen?*' Tom shouted to Sue as she bolted in through the front door to escape the rain.

'C-O-N,' Sue called back. 'Why?'

'No, not that. The port up North – I'm trying to book a ferry, you silly cow! You remember, we're supposed to be going back to the UK for the big game and a bit of a jolly. Why that face?'

'It's the only one I have. Listen Tom, I don't think the trip's gonna happen. There are things going on . . . things, well, um, that we need to discuss. We've got to sort out a few details, so come in the kitchen and I'll make some tea.'

Sue's unusually resigned tone made Tom take note, and he felt the atmosphere in the house suddenly tighten with a terrible tension. He wrapped up his rambling computer research and padded over into the farmhouse kitchen.

Sue was efficiently placing tea bags into mugs and lifting milk from the fridge. She got straight to the point, and as it wasn't going to be an easy one, she had decided to take the bull by the horns and say what had to be said, desperate to leave Tom and return to Claude as soon as reasonably possible.

'I'm afraid we've come to the end of the road, Tom. It's over between us. You know, it's pretty obvious that we've reached an impasse in our relationship. Whatever was there once has long gone, as you well know, and anyway . . . well, anyway, I've met someone else who's really special to me and . . .' she tailed off, faltering.

The inevitable cliché-rich break up chat ensued, the usual petty gripes and niggling regrets, sore jealousies and insecurities rising unnecessarily to the fore. Sue was exhausted yet exhilarated when she finally managed to tear herself away a good hour later, dragging the weight of a heavy suitcase, crunching stone en route to the car, but with a different weight off her shoulders and another life left behind her. Pausing briefly behind the wheel in order to gather her thoughts, she found the silence of the countryside intolerable until the car coughed into life, but couldn't deny herself a half smile as she meandered down the track to start a new adventure in her life.

'A fucking French fucking farming frog fucking farmer, for Chrissake! What the fuck? It's not like he's young, popular, rich, good-looking, talented, or even fucking English, and . . . and he looks like his face has been splashed with acid! It looks fucking half-finished, like the sculptor ran out of clay and time. Fuck! I should've suspected something when the pube trimmer turned up from Amazon, it certainly wasn't for my benefit. Disingenuous cow! And all the bloody new lotions and potions . . . There's me, there's always me . . .' Tom swayed. 'I've always been there, it's me, Tom. You're bloody emotionally autistic. Well fuck you, then, you're a fake anyway, a fake. You're the kind of woman who wastes our money buying a load of fruit just to make the kitchen look good, like in a fucking magazine, to impress guests or whatever when they come over. Then you slowly let it all go off without even touching it. A bit like our relationship, you've let it fucking well go off! A lime. Beautiful and fresh-looking, but when cut in half you find that it's all shrivelled and dry. Well, that's her! Oh, shit, it's me, it's me! It's your Tom.' Seriously drunk now and throwing red wine down his neck as if it were beer, he was feeling miserably sorry for himself. They had split up before years previously, but he'd always been sure that it would be temporary, and it had been. This time there was another man, and it felt finished and final . . . and fucked.

The run of prison gigs had been going well for the The Prison Breakers, with the bookings rolling in from Her Majesty's Prison Service, an unlikely but reliable benefactor. Still, even a band like this could have its own in-fighting and politics that sometimes would ruin one of their trips. Much more damaging than a personal comment about someone's appearance or bodily aroma would be a detrimental remark concerning their playing or musicianship. Will had been feeling increasingly paranoid that he wasn't wanted anymore in the group, and he was right. Baz and T had become a lot more matey with Dave who ran the outfit, and Will's guitar talents were not appreciated much anymore. Baz had complained that his timing was suspect, adding to Dave that 'his feel sucks, man. He just doesn't have it, and it's just all the wrong vibe, you know. His groove doesn't fit and it ain't sittin' in the pocket, man. He never gets the right sound out of that axe, I reckon he doesn't have a clue about his effects pedals . . . ' and it went on. Baz had been abroad once, on a five-day trip to Normandy with his parents when he was 12. He still insisted however on attempting to speak as if he had been brought up in New Orleans by black American jazz-club-owning parents. T was putting the boot in too, 'why can't he turn down? I'm always saying it, and he doesn't get it, you know what I'm sayin'? I don't think he ever listens to the rest of us, he's up there doing his own thing in his little world, he thinks he's in a fookin' busy pizza restaurant strumming away all that shite. And the gobshite wears his gay-tar far too fookin' high – does he think we're some gay fookin' jazz/fusion combo from the 80s?'

Just as those words were uttered was the moment that Will clambered back into the packed van with a coffee, clamping a slightly warm and disappointingly limp and clammy Ginsters pasty into his mouth as he slammed the sliding door shut. 'Talking about me again, are we?' he blurted out through a mouthful of pitiful pastry. 'All good I hope? This service station is shit and the bogs . . . uuuggghhhh!'

He had no idea. Dave had made up his mind: he'd let Will do the gigs that he'd booked him for, that was another three, and he'd sack him face to face after the HMP Isle of Wight gig which was a few weeks away. He'd have to brief the other guys not to mention any other gigs, or future plans, so he could steer clear from potentially awkward conversations. Dave tucked into his giant Scotch egg bought from a deli near his house that morning, a speciality item that was nearly the size of a baby's brain, although not particularly a similar texture. He had nearly chosen the goat's cheese, bacon and fresh basil focaccia, but the deli owner's cute daughter had been pushing the Scotch eggs, and he had fallen under her spell. Tinny music on the radio stopped briefly as a brash and overpaid DJ shouted something about someone having won a competition. The prize was a mug. 'Bloody hell, must be a recession on. I'm sure people used to win a grand!' Will piped up. Nobody answered him and nobody laughed.

THE AMAZING EX

Burgled by a bastard
I've so little to say,
Our world keeps on turning
He'll get it one day.

She cheats just so casually,
Apparently without guilt
Which side tells the lies
Is it Miss Jekyll or Miss Hyde?

The little children, they suffer
Still, she doesn't care
Just checks what's on offer to
Bring back to her lair.
If she cannot realise her
Great Big Mistake, whether
Mental or Evil, it's
Already too late.

The lies that she tells have
Dark, disturbing smells
To think that once upon a time
I found her so fine!

If you've learnt from such a tale
That it's hard to be a male
I've had my say,
Should I try to be gay!?

By Yatter

Paul's Nazi stash was in need of a major rearrangement as a couple of probing enquiries had been made by a rather secretive gentleman from Leeds who 'may well be paying the shop a visit in the not too distant future with a view to picking up some important historical items'. Such interest in this genre of material had become almost a fetish for some, one of the prizes being a first edition of *Mein Kampf*, which could command some serious money. The front door's latch was on and Paul was clumsily clambering across boxes in the back room. It had slipped his mind to call Foul Fred about shifting the transsexual and animal porn stash, and he remembered suddenly on almost tripping over it. 'Must give Fred a ding,' he mumbled, steadying himself on a life-sized reproduction Greek garden figure of a naked man. Ray Charles' tones tickled the tweeters and children laughed as they messed about outside on their way home from school. He stooped down to pull back bubble wrap protruding from a shabby Pickfords cardboard box, torn across the top. A heavy-looking hardback book was sat on the top, adorned with a colourful dust cover. He picked it up slowly: Nazi Occult, Magic & Science Fiction. Another book underneath was all about insignia and uniforms. There were strange Nazi-inspired novels imagining modern life if the Germans had won WWII, along with bizarre Nazi Science Fiction paperbacks, with lurid titles such as *Master Race in Space, Panzers Patrol Pluto, SS Slav Sex Slaves, Gestapo Japes around Jupiter, U-Boat Babe in Port* and *Lunar Death Camp.* One specialized publication that concentrated solely on SS staff cars appeared to have been heavily read with its ragged and well-thumbed pages, and there was an unusually slim edition tucked down the side that Paul almost didn't notice: a detailed account of her war years by Himmler's masseuse. At the bottom of the box, wrapped in a dirty towel, Paul found the Luger pistol that he was looking for. Satisfied, he repacked the box and humped it over to the side, so he could pull out another one. This was marked DELICATE, and he was pretty sure it was the right one. An abrupt tearing crack reverberated sharply around the room as Paul fought his way through tough tape securing the contents. Ripping away yellowing pages of the *Daily Mail* from years before, he carefully held up the top item – a serving platter from a full dinner service with gold leaf all around the rim, the Nazi eagle and swastika emblem prominently displayed just above the centre. He admired it and let out a prolonged sigh.

'I Wonder Who's Kissin' Her Now?' Ray Charles sang as Paul slowly moistened his lips, running his index finger lovingly over the sickening emblem. He often spoke out loud to himself as he spent so much time alone.

'I'm going to miss you, you beauty, and your friends. You make sure you go to a welcoming home. You never know, you might even get displayed or used, just like back in the good ol' days.' He hesitated for a moment, before packing up the two boxes and secreting them under the counter in the front room, tucked away in the safety and darkness of the corner.

Just as he finished, and seemingly from nowhere, a vivid memory flashed into Paul's brain. He was back in the forest playing army games with his neighbours Jack and Alan; they couldn't have all been much more than 8 years old. They pinned him down by them and for what seemed like hours pointed a pistol right into the bridge of his nose really hard while screaming at him again and again, 'You will die prisoner, you will be shot!' He could sense an unconditional power over him, and feel the spittle flying out of their mouths onto his face as hatred came hurtling towards him with the incessant shouting. They had only left him alone after he pissed his pants and started to cry. Paul remembered their bitter laughter as they ran off to go home for tea, leaving him in the woods soaking wet with urine and tears cascading down his cheeks.

Paul suddenly didn't feel right, and the hairs were standing up on his forearms. He felt chilly. He returned to the boxes and pulled out a small magazine destined for Foul Fred. Then he pulled out a few more, opened them up and spread them around on the tops of boxes with one hand, as he started to undo his belt with the other. Six minutes and forty-eight seconds later there was an unsettling animalistic cry that poisoned the back room of the shop as the sixty-year-old Paul roughly brought himself to orgasm over one of the magazines, followed by a sharp sigh. 'You can Fuck Off, an' all!' he spat up at the the Greek statue that appeared to be spying on him. He half-heartedly mopped up the majority of the mess that he'd made, and returned his vile appendage back inside his trousers whilst deciding to close early and go to the pub.

HAPPY CHRISTMAS FROM THE JONES FAMILY!!!

We'd all love to take this opportunity to wish you all the very best Festive Greetings, whilst also keeping you up to date with our Family events and our achievements over the last twelve months. It has been a year of ups and downs. But mainly ups!!!!!! We are all immensely proud of Gerry who managed to get a 2:1 in Molecular Science at Northampton University, and we're all hoping that he's possibly starting to think about perhaps getting a job sometime in the not too distant future!!!!!! Unfortunately Stanley suffered a second stroke back in February, as many of you will know, but he is recovering well and battling on. Thanks to God for the health service over here. Onwards and Upwards!!!!!! Rachel spent most of the summer in Ibiza, and reports back that she enjoyed a drink or two!!!!!! She's still got a lovely tan and is in good spirits. I've been busy at the shop, although I've cut down on the hours to look after Stanley a little more. The dishwasher broke in May, but now Stanley's around more I've got a new one, he even puts the plates away!!!! Of course I still enjoy the Choral Society, and am still enjoying my role as Secretary. I'm certain that it'd fall apart if I wasn't there for Gordon!!!!!! We do actually get some singing done from time to time as well!!!!!! Our May concert was a resounding success, we had an impressive 54 people in the audience, and a lot of French friends came along too to support us, which was nice!!!!! Buster our loving dog is fine, and he still keeps us fit with his walks!!!!!! Tess the crazy cat is the same as ever, jumping over that back wall still and frightening us all, we love her!!!!!! The extension that we had planned to build over the Spring/Summer has been put on hold, but we might be starting something next year, so don't be surprised if you bump into us down one of the aisles at a DIY store soon!! So as you can see we've had an eventful year, and we are hoping and praying that your year next year will be as good as our year was this year!!!!! Happy Christmas to You All, Onwards and Upwards! love from Margery, Stanley, Gerry and Rachel Jones xxxx

'It's fucking September and those idiot expats neighbours are sending Christmas cards out with this fucking Round Robin family bulletin shit inside on a bit of A4, like we give a shit! What the fuck is this?!' Tom's rant had started over the morning post. He fidgeted uncomfortably, scrunching the paper up, then tossed it aside with a sneer.

'Who gives a fuck? I hardly know them. The summer's not even over and they think it's fuckin' Christmas? I don't even know them and they think I'm fucking interested? The only reason I even acknowledge them is 'cos I sometimes like to jump in their swimming pool if it's baking hot! They think that putting more exclamation marks at the end of a crap joke might make it funny? NO! Cunts.'

Tom was addressing Keith who'd popped over mid-morning with some croissants, still warm. If Tom thought that this envelope bearing a ridiculously early Christmas card from his nearest English neighbours would annoy him, he clearly hadn't noticed the handwriting on one of the other letters. It was from Sue. In fact, it was from Sue and Claude.

He picked it up and waited a second or two before slowly tearing the back, almost whistling as he extracted the note and straightened up to take it in.

Dear Tom,

It's been quite a few weeks now, and we haven't managed to have a proper chat about the future. Claude and I have decided that we are getting married, so I'd like to arrange a divorce with you.

I am going to the UK shortly, so I will organise an appointment with a Solicitor then, and you will receive a letter soon.

I hope that you're doing well and are okay.

Sue & Claude.

'For bastard's shitting sake, mate, she's only gonna fuckin' marry the cunt. She's taken a shit in our family's kitchen sink with this affair . . . pissed on the living room floor, and now this. She's fucking off to the UK . . . oh, fuck mate, let's fuck these croissants off and grab us a beer out of the fridge will you?'

Tom had a face like a wet weekend. 'Jesus, I haven't told you, I just found out yesterday that old Auntie Mildred – bless her little cotton socks – went to bed with her hot water bottle and the fuckin' thing only went and leaked everywhere – she probably thought she'd pissed herself at first! She burnt herself quite badly though, then went and fuckin' electrocuted herself on the wet electric blanket as she was trying to jump out of bed. Brown bread, mate. She was only sixty-nine. Let's get pissed.'

Even at this early hour Keith was easily persuaded to assist his friend in his time of need, scuttling across to the beer fridge. Tom's eyes were welling up, but he didn't want Keith to notice. He concentrated instead on his pounding red-wine hangover, unforgiving asbestos mouth and the uneasy sense of not belonging and falling apart that ensued after such a monumental emotional shock. He had spent the previous evening miserably festering on his own, half-watching cheap reality

TV shows while dispatching three bottles of local plonk. With no recollection of going to bed, he had woken early feeling parched, guilty and like a broken man. A UDI (*Unidentified Drinking Injury*) on his left flank throbbed rhythmically, a blueish bruise that was set to spread. He pushed his half-empty coffee mug away dismissively, ignoring the delicious croissants in their warm paper bag, and with a theatrical sweep eagerly ripped the ring off the ice-cold beer that Keith had fetched.

'Fuck 'em all!' he toasted Keith with false confidence.

'Fuck 'em all!' Keith replied, aiming to maintain a similar upbeat tone in his delivery. 'It's an early but welcome brew, and you know what they say: it's past midday somewhere in the world! Anyhow, it says on this tin 'Established 1856' and I was born in 1956, so I'm clearly meant to represent and celebrate their centenary, cheers!'

'Oh wait,' Tom added, raising his can skywards again, 'here's to Mildred the ol' dear, who went out with a bang!' The two men cackled like a pair of scheming witches.

'Listen, Tom,' said Keith. His expression became suddenly serious. 'There's an old African proverb, which goes something like this: *it's not until the peacock feeds from the dead that you realise that it's actually a vulture*. You have to look at the positive side, maybe you got out of this one just fine, you just don't know it yet.'

Tom swigged deep from the can before fixing his drinking buddy with a huge forced smile, giving nothing away. Keith went on, 'Everyone has a temper to a certain degree, the trick is to know how not to lose it.' He felt good giving advice, helping Tom in his hour of need, the constantly elevated level of alcohol in his bloodstream loosening his tongue.

'Yeah, well, that's all very reasonable. I've got a bit of a situation with the bloody pigeons and slugs out the back there, they're really beginning to piss me off too,' Tom added.

Keith seemed to have an answer for everything today: 'Still, you see how it's all good – if it was rats and fleas it'd be much worse!'

Keith the alcoholic. He loved nothing more than to sit watching the Grand Prix or football, generous drink in hand, his wife's oversize nightie warming on the electric radiator by the TV wafting her scent, emitting a sense of comfort, the fat flea-ridden cat sat square in the middle of their dining table aside the salt and pepper, smells of yet more fried food drifting over the kitchen bar towards him. The exact alcohol type or quality he imbibed had little relevance: beer, wine or spirits. There was no pattern or set attitude towards this, except the fact that it would have to be both cheap and plentiful. Pure comfort. It saddened Keith to see his friend in such a state, but he wouldn't let him down. On the contrary, Keith would stand side by side with Tom, man to man, and drink as much as Tom needed, and at whatever time, to help him. After all, they were mates, and that's what mates do, right? They stick together, and if Tom wanted to drink himself ragged every day, then Keith would make it his mission to join him, to support his buddy.

By the time evening came the two drinking men still hadn't eaten. The cuckolded drunk was nearly dribbling. 'Every time now that I think about . . . *that woman* . . . a four-letter word crosses my mind, and it starts with a C and ends in a T.'

'What could that be? *Curt* ? Does she have a rather curt manner?' japed Keith.

'Yeah, right,' laughed Tom.

'Or is it *Curd* ? Is she a fan of lemon curd?'

'Not quite! Anyway, you messed up there, that's a D on the end of Curd!' corrected Tom.

'Oh, yeah, you're right.'

'No, it's a bit ruder than that . . .'

'Hey, I've got it . . . it's *Clit*!' Keith was triumphant.

'No, you idiot!'

'Ok, wait, wait . . . ' Keith wouldn't stop, he was on a roll.

'You *Can't* put the *Coot* in the *Cart* with your arm in a *Cast*, so she had an affair, it's simple!'

'You really are a prize knob!' remarked Tom. They both chuckled.

A short while later, Tom was off again. 'They're like wine . . . good for a few days but they go off after a while. Jesus, can't live with them, can't shoot 'em. All women baffle me, always have. Fucking enigmas, enigmas they are, all women, all of them. You know, people think that we argue, well, they're wrong . . . *she* argues. I try to be nice and when I'm kind it just goes down like a rat sandwich. It's been like living with an annoying flatmate you don't even like, all wrong. She's bloody emotionally autistic. Jekyll and Hyde shit, you see, she saves the soft, smiling, fun side for everybody else and all I get is aggression and nasty anger. What a bitch, like a mosquito in December . . . a rare pain in the arse! Oh fuck, she's even left all her shit here, I'm actually using her padded bra as a cradle for my mobile phone when I charge it upstairs – it's perfect!' Tom went on, and on. 'You know, these French, they're pretty clued up on things. I mean, they even told Sue the other day that she couldn't give blood over here because of Mad Cow's Disease . . . well, they got that spot on, didn't they, mate? Anyway, enough about me, let's talk about . . . me!'

A while later: 'My heart has been kicked and trampled like a friggin' rugby ball since the moment that I was born, even if it's just a muscle which will repair, eventually. What's so damn special about her, anyhow? She thinks she's special, better, above us, you know? She's mean and shallow, I've taken a fucking bath deeper than her! Hey, did you know that there's no French word for shallow, when talking about water at least? They just say, *not very deep*! Well, too bad, because if – or when – the *Titanic* sinks, it'll take everyone down with it even those fuckers travelling in First Class. She doesn't understand me . . . never will . . .' he drunkenly droned.

Unusually, the final tone of this particular drinking session was pretty downbeat and morose, and they weren't even winding each other up for a laugh, as usual. Keith – not really listening to Tom's miserable outpourings any more – was off on another tangent. 'I'm a bit worried that when I get to heaven there'll be no beer and cigars,' he considered.

Keith was getting bored, and quite drunk. 'Listen Tom,' he slurred finally, a perfectly rounded drip of watery snot balancing dangerously off the tip of his nose, 'I'd better be getting back to the Mrs, I don't want her thinking that I'm pissed or anything. See you soon, mate. Chin up!'

'Okay, fella. Scratch your crater.'

'What?!' uttered Keith, balancing precariously on an arm of a chair as he raised himself up to go.

'Catch you later!' explained Tom as they both snorted drunkenly.

'Excrement!' returned Keith on his wobbly journey to the door.

It was 7:48 p.m. when Keith staggered home. His face was resplendent in all its sebaceous glory, forehead shiny like cheap kebab meat. He had yet to eat anything, but had managed to match Tom beer by beer, a respectable total of sixteen 500ml cans of 5.2% strength lager. 'Hi darling,' he blurted out optimistically as he fell in the musty porch of the marital home, sending some empty bottle-bank-ready bottles flying with a crash. 'Are you cooking?'

I am floating and can smell food being cooked on a barbecue. Ah, there is Rick Astley with a chef's pinafore on, sporting a chef's hat perched on his spectacularly bouffant hair. I am enraptured at once, yet feel completely at ease in his presence.

RA: *If we were together in a train carriage, Ahmed, then perhaps I could serve you sausages with mustard in the buffet car? Do you think they'd mind if I set up my barbecue in the buffet car?*

Ahmed: I'm sure that shouldn't be a problem, Rick. I would imagine that the train people would bend over backwards for somebody of your stature, Rick.

RA: *Well, then. I'd be more than happy to serve you several sausages with mustard in the buffet car of the train, Ahmed. In fact, it would give me great pleasure to do so. However, there is a minor task that you must carry out in return, before I will consider doing so.*

Ahmed: Anything for you Rick, anything. I wish for nothing else but to be served meat and mustard by you in the buffet car, Rick. What is it that you're thinking about, Rick?

RA: *My desire is that you blow up the train, Ahmed. Yes, you. Yes, you yourself and a bomb. Yes, you and a bomb that you will make yourself. This is what I require of you, Ahmed. I know that you are capable, and that you are the right man for the job. You have been chosen, by no mere coincidence. This you will do for our friends and for the cause that we both know is right. If you grant my simple request then I will furnish you with many hot sausages, all splashed liberally with fine mustard, Ahmed, served just the way that I know you like them.*

Ahmed: I am your servant, Rick. I aim to please, so the train will be attacked. I must prepare, mentally and physically.

Ahmed woke up with a start, drenched in sweat and feeling shaky. His penis throbbed and almost hurt as it pushed hard into his polyester trousers, but there was distinct pleasure there too. He was starving. All that he could hear was that rhythmic metallic jangling of a trolley being roughly shoved along the pavement outside, urgently propelling its packaged bullets of lemonade and ginger beer towards the newsagent on the corner. As the noise subsided, it reminded him of a train pulling away and off into the distant countryside. The neighbours must be having a barbecue, he could smell animal cooking over fire, and it made him ravenous like Prehistoric Man. His erection quickly subsided, and he frowned as he pulled himself up off the couch and shoved Elvis gently to wake him. 'Come on, boy, we've got work to do.' The shabby dog half-heartedly raised his head before he flopped down and sleep was achieved once again. Ahmed left him, wandering into the kitchen to make a mug of coffee. While the kettle boiled he moved over to the computer tower and belted the keyboard, the screen lighting up instantly as a soft whirring sound emanated from deep within the plastic casing. There were five emails:

14:07. Viagra Direct: 4 for the price of 3 discount, right now you will receive an outstanding . . .
13:24. Pam's Pizzas: it's time to celebrate this weekend in style with our great offers on . . .
13:21. Kenny G Newsletter: keep up to date with all Kenny's latest tour dates and recordings, with . . .
13:13. The Bobby Davro Fan Club: why not re-subscribe to receive more fantastic news and . . .
12:50. Friend from Overseas: Ahmed, you have been chosen and are ready for the mission . . .

Ahmed blinked hard before clicking precisely on the last message. He read his instructions slowly, hardly able to believe that he had been selected so soon, and for such an important job. After re-reading the long email a couple of times, Ahmed sat, almost still, on the couch for ten minutes. He forgot about the coffee. All that he could do was think, but however much he attempted to clear his mind and focus, it was racing with all the excitement of the task in hand. An angst-induced tightness at once knotted his stomach. The message explained how their God had guided him to them, and that he was not alone, he was among friends. It was to be a train that he would bomb, as in the dream. Everything was coming together and making perfect sense. Things were shaping up, just in the right way, giving Ahmed purpose. Eventually he decided that he must go for a walk to calm himself. He shook the dog as it yawned itself awake, foul breath pouring over Ahmed's pores.

'Come on, Elvis, walkies!'

Once outside, the pair of them felt fresh from sleep, invigorated and eager to explore. 'Elvis has left the building!' chuckled Ahmed as they made their way up the short garden path (his standard joke nearly every time they left the house). It was a damp yet pleasing Autumn afternoon that smelt of gingerbread and bonfire. It wasn't spitting or pissing, but rather *crying* rain, just enough to placate the local farmers. In front of the newsagent lay three sad newspapers cynically on a plastic stand, somehow refusing to blow in the breeze. MCN (*Motorcycle News*) nestled alongside *Loot* (only £1.60), which slightly obscured the headline of *The Irish Times.*

Ahmed informed Elvis, 'Whatever newspaper you care to read, all that's for certain is that the truth will be in the *other* newspaper that you didn't buy.' Elvis didn't reply.

They marched on past the newsagent's sorry fruit display and the blackened bags of charcoal towards the grey town centre, a copycat blueprint of any mid-sized urban centre anywhere in the country. Ahmed scoffed at a fluorescent yellow poster tastelessly plastered on a board adorning the side of a Norman church: *The Best Vitamin for a Christian is* B1. And alongside it in fluorescent pink: *Give the Devil an Inch and he will become your Ruler.*

'Idiots!' He scowled into the wind. 'We can't ever escape the sight of a church, anywhere in this country, even in the smallest village. Just there to influence and dictate to us, Elvis, spires and towers everywhere. This Christian State, I spit on you!' Onwards they strolled into town, past the crumbling 60s concrete leisure centre. A decrepit looking woman with wet hair, dressed head to toe in Slazenger sports gear, swept out through the revolving door and professionally sparked up a Richmond Gold Superking (100mm of cigarette) with her yellow Bic lighter (standard range). She glanced over and almost smiled at Elvis. They carried on past the Victorian NHS hospice, formerly called The Hospital for Incurables.

Apparently, nobody should call it that anymore, but it (perhaps) unfortunately remains etched into the huge stone lintel above the main gate for all to clearly see as they enter the premises. Outside he noticed a gaggle of young girls hanging around the bus stop, clearly dressed to go out on the town. They were already drinking their pre-pre-club tinnies, while sharing long drags on cigarettes and talking about TV and boys.

'Look at that lot,' Ahmed confided in Elvis. 'That's how you end up pregnant at fifteen, that is. We need to teach these people, we *must* teach them. It's changed from Paradise to Hell.'

Whistling tunelessly, the Schoolboy Jihadist suddenly felt empowered like never before. He wanted to shout out aloud for everyone to hear, but instead he quietly explained everything to Elvis as they strolled through Aldershot town, passing a buzzing café where some over-enthusiastic 30-somethings were high-5-ing noisily as if they were in an episode of *Friends*.

'All of these infidels are complicit in their Government's actions against us – they know what's going on, they all have TVs and watch the news, read newspapers and surf the internet. They are as guilty as the politicians and the soldiers. It's the democratically-elected governments who wage this constant crusade against us, and we will fight back. We are just defending our religion and our Muslim brothers and sisters – it was these people that brought the war to us, not the other way around. Our Crusade will have the upper hand, we will retaliate against the evil Westerners. The enlightened and true believer like myself will avenge my fellow people, and I have chosen principles over fear. Let evil into your heart and it will make its home there. You know, none of these feeble people passing by have any inkling of how important and great I have become. They barely glance at me, and don't even recognize my existence, but my impact on many lives will be far greater than that which any of these miserable mortals will ever achieve. I am part of Generation Jihad, and will be the harbinger of things to come whose name will not be lost in time. But all these words are dead until we give them life with our blood, just like the infidel Crusaders did when they roasted babies on spits. Years of mediocrity in my world has no relevance any more, and nothing needs pinpointing or considering except my upcoming mission, and Elvis, it's gonna be something to remember, you'll see. We'll make them realise exactly how pathetic their lives have become, Elvis, we'll show them.'

Ahmed surprised himself with this outburst, and suddenly realised quite how hungry he had become, so they doubled back to take the last free outside table at the café they had already passed, after deciding against the fish 'n' chip place The Codfather. He decided to initiate a blindingly simple yet hugely tasty and effective hunger-release operation that involved a plate of bangers and mash. Ahmed adored this humble nostalgia-inducing British Classic meal that nearly always hit the mark, as long as the sausages were up to standard of course, as well as the chef. Just as he had chosen, the waitress hurried out of the kitchen to deliver a plate of overpriced dry ham and limp-looking vegetables to an ageing gentleman in the corner, and a bowl of whitebait to his wife. 'Mass murder in a bowl!' Ahmed mouthed to Elvis with a smile. The young man at the next table nervously checked his phone every few seconds while stuffing a burger into his mouth, eating heavily.

Ahmed considering it strange that he could eat this and a plate of chips without any drink, not even water. A couple of hipsters who would look more at home in Camden-on-Sea (otherwise known as Brighton) were enjoying each other's company after a raucous night out in Aldershot's latest addition to the club scene, The Closet, whose advertising tag line is *If Gay's your Way then That's OK!*. The older one, who was wearing a haggard look and appeared bored, was camply sipping soup as the other talked at him, apparently even without pausing for breath and eager to please. Two teenage girls were earnestly tucking into enormous knickerbocker glories despite the weather. A baby slept in a dirty pushchair between them, probably another human to continue the great tradition of the 30-year-old grandmother, which seemed to be all the rage in this town. Ahmed peered over his shoulder, eventually managing to grab the attention of the waitress, and although she was exceedingly pleasing on the eye he appeared not to notice.

'Hello, there. Could I have the sausages and mash, please? Oh, and a glass of tap water. And don't forget the mustard . . . that's very important,' he explained with a slight chuckle that ended in a snort.

'Of course, no problem.' The young waitress scurried away, a slight frown furrowing her silky brow.

'Mustard for his sausages . . . okay, sir!' she muttered under her breath, scribbling on her impossibly tiny notepad. *Mustard for the freak*, she jotted down.

In what seemed to him like only a minute or two, his lunch arrived, slid in front of him as the girl hurried away with a much-rehearsed 'enjoy!' The chef clearly suffered from the disease of portion distortion and intended to spread it to his customers, and Ahmed imagined him to be a fat man. There were three huge sausages sticking upwards rudely out of a dollop of lumpy mash the size of a grapefruit, all swimming in a glistening gravy lake. As Ahmed meticulously ploughed his way through the food, a carnivorous success, he pondered his mission. This was to be his last meal for now, as he would fast for 24 hours in order to cleanse himself and direct his energy and thoughts to how he would carry out the plan of building and planting a bomb on a passenger train somewhere in the UK. This was real life, and his Destiny was certain. He had never once imagined that he may check out this early in life, but his time had come and his pride swelled with the thought. It dawned on him that he hadn't felt this optimistic about anything before, an excitement like electricity buzzing through his nerves and filling him with a triumphant sense of urgency.

All of a sudden a wasp appeared from over his shoulder and dramatically crash landed on his plate, falling out of control like a disabled plane struck violently in a storm and tumbling to Earth . Still alive but clearly stunned, it gingerly moved forwards until it made contact with the periphery of a puddle of dark gravy by the mound of mashed potato, which, to the insect, must have resembled an enormous dirty lake alongside a towering mountain of snow. Ahmed grimaced, his eyes narrowing as he pushed the wasp into the gravy with his fork and applied a slight pressure on the defenceless insect until its exoskeleton cracked audibly. The large metal fork then pressed down onto the hard china, precisely separating the insect's head from the mesosoma, then the mesosoma from the striped metasoma. It was only then that the frantic and almost mechanical movement of the legs halted as the dissected and semi-squashed abdomen parts were covered in lukewarm packet sauce.

'It's a one-way ticket, mate. You've gone in there and there's no coming back,' Ahmed said to himself and the wasp as he pushed the plate across the table, his soft crush fetish satiated, the surgery complete. One morning, as an acne-ridden teenager, he had rescued an earthworm. Later that same damp day he was coming home to RonJoyce with his parents, his dad behind the wheel of their cream Toyota Corolla 1400, registration number TEP 793V. (NB: The Corolla was the classic functional domestic family vehicle, not in the same league as the stunning Toyota Hilux which rose like a phoenix through the years to become the preferred model of choice for any self-respecting modern-day Islamic terrorist.) They had pulled over after Peter had seen a cat on the side of the road and had insisted on stopping to check that the feline was okay – which it certainly wasn't. It had been hit by a car at a previous undefined moment in time and was fully rigamortified, a wax-like globular beard bright red under broken mouth. The journey home was resumed in a respectful silence. A few minutes further up the road, his dad was unable to avoid a small deer which had materialised from nowhere. Result: one very dead deer and a cracked headlight casing, decorated with warm animal blood. If they hadn't had pulled over for the cat, they wouldn't have hit the deer . . . but could something *worse* have occurred instead? This sudden memory provoked Ahmed's thoughts once again.

'You take a risk every single miserable day of your life just by falling out of bed and getting up in the morning. Let's look at this rationally . . . I mean, you could easily choke on your morning banana, couldn't you? We don't all die peacefully in our sleep at the age of 87 surrounded by our loving family, do we? What the people have to understand at the end of the day is that it's all about life, and life is about destroying things: livers, lungs, relationships, tribes, animal species, the environment . . .' he paused '. . . *lives*.' Ahmed's left eyelid shook suddenly and uncontrollably, and, once irritated, he stood up, waving a £10 note at the waitress. The atmosphere changed for Ahmed then and there, he shivered, and wanted to get back to the warmth and comforting familiarity of RonJoyce.

'Imagine if there was a bomb scare here right now, wouldn't that be great?' He smiled to nobody, and nobody smiled back. He paid without leaving a tip and hurried home, picking up a box of Medjool dates from the newsagent on the corner as he passed (origin: the Boudenib oasis, Morocco). *Eat the Rich* had been sprayed boldly over an advertising hoarding for the new Skoda estate. This made Ahmed frown. He found himself fumbling with the keys and let Elvis through the front door, judging that his vegetables didn't need watering as a distinct gloom now presided over the afternoon and a satisfying constant drizzle peppered his garden. Once inside, he was instantly comforted by the familiar warming aroma of RonJoyce, a mixture of general dog smell and damp carpet. The hallway had suffered from rising damp for as long as he could remember, and having grown accustomed to it, he found no reason to ever deal with it. Ahmed opened up his parent's old record player (a treasured Philips 9573a), half itched and half stroked his rampant beard, and put on *The 100 Most Relaxing Classical Themes . . . Ever!* before flopping down onto the sofa next to Elvis. Now he would fast for 24 hours to clear his head, in order to fully concentrate on the task in hand.

THE HANDICAPPED FLY

She felt useless, incapable, as if
Showing her vagina to a homosexual man could achieve
More, and activate a secret plan.
Life was passing her by, and she felt
Useless, incapable, like a fly . . . no better than a
Handicapped Fly.

By Yatter

Norman had made up his mind. India was beckoning, and he needed a plane ticket. After picking up an Evening Standard that afternoon on his way back from the supermarket, he'd pinpointed a couple of adverts for flights towards the sports section at the end of the paper. 'Mumbai from £199 Return' screamed the letters. '2 weeks in Goa from £289' he had circled with one of Yatter's biros emblazoned with a motorbike courier-company logo. Norman's knowledge of computers was negligible, and the last laptop that he had bought was flickering erratically like a strobe light with a ropey plug. If he ever were to locate the receipt – which of course he never would as his life was in constant disarray – he would have found that the machine was two days past its guarantee date anyway. So, he picked up the cordless phone and tapped away, the old-fashioned way. Number unavailable. He tried again. It rang for a while before an answerphone message kicked in: '. . . the premier ticket agency for your exotic holiday destination . . . Crest of a Wave Flights, the premier ticket agency for your exotic holiday destination . . . please wait and one of our friendly operators will be with you shortly . . . Crest of a Wave Flights, the premier ticket agency to suit all your holiday needs . . .'

Norman's brow furrowed and he jerkily itched a mole on his neck as he waited. Then he scratched at a minor irritation on the back of his left knee. Seven minutes thirty-eight seconds later, a tired male voice punctuated the overly upbeat female tones of the message, cutting off the now all-too-familiar recording.

'Hullo, Crest of a Wave, can I help you?'

'Oh, hi. Yes, yes I'm looking for a flight to Bombay – I mean Mumbai. Anytime in the next month for a couple of weeks will do, just find me a cheap option, please.'

'Ok, uh . . . just hold on a moment,' the salesman mumbled. '. . . one minute . . . here we are, the cheapest is to depart Gatwick at 3:30 a.m. next Sunday, and the return from Mumbai leaves 4:50 a.m. on the Sunday two weeks later, and the price is only £847. Sorry, that's £847 plus taxes and some extras, plus a small booking fee and of course a credit card charge. Would you like to go ahead with that one?'

The Electric Dwarf was puzzled. Had the advert not promised a return flight for £199? The explanation:

'Ah, yes sir. I'm afraid that this price is a very occasional promotion which we don't appear to be able to access currently. The wording says *from* £199 I believe, not *for* £199.'

Norman's mind drifted towards the world of international travel: where had the glamour gone? Every Tom, Dick and Harry flies these days, apparently. From what he could make out it was now all about angry queues, cheap-looking garish hostess uniforms, having to present your boarding pass to buy a 49p pack of tissues, the 6 a.m. pint of Stella Artois – an obligatory badge of honour for the working man starting his hard-earned foreign holiday – the eager young couple canoodling, stressed young mum juggling two toddlers who take turns throwing tantrums, the fidgeting woman with the Bisto tan standing in line while desperate for the toilet, a faint yet constant background hum of vomit, the neighbouring passenger who aggressively occupies all the arm rest between you at all times, the aggressively sunburnt bunch of weary girls coming back from a hen party, grim nuclear food that burns the roof of your mouth or over-priced dry sandwiches, a cranky PA system that forces you to listen to inane musak before blasting out announcements at an ear-splitting volume, the surly Lithuanian hostess (or is she Croatian, Bulgarian, Hungarian or maybe Latvian?), some weird small advance payment on self-printed boarding pass for the advantage of getting on the plane before others (some sort of poor-man's first class?), the complimentary crash landing courtesy of Ryanair, the amazing blue lane at Customs where you don't even have to declare whether or not you have anything to declare (to be designated to history after Brexit no doubt; we'll be left with the much less cool green or red decision), intrusive wafts of body odour as the slightly panting overweight gentleman shuffles past up the aisle whilst brushing past dozing passengers on his mission to the galley to request more nuts and a Coke, the Ryanair cold which can never be shaken off, the people who don't know how to travel (abstractly blocking doors and escalators/ stopping abruptly in corridors and ambling stupidly etc. etc.), the bored Pakistani-British Border Control Officer with his glistening forehead slowly leafing through the passport pages, deliberately taking his time as the weary line of passengers shift their weight from foot to foot and stand obediently in line. . .

He eventually agreed on a ticket which cost him dear and

was decided upon more through exhaustion than choice, paid by credit card then put the kettle on. Not for the first time, as the water came to a rolling boil, the Electric Dwarf rolled a fat spliff in celebration. The funny little man was brimming with a sense of anticipation as he propped the neatly bulging white stick in the ashtray's groove and stood up to make a strong mug of sweet tea, the tried and tested ideal companion to a relaxing afternoon joint. He zapped the TV on and sat down to watch Sly Stallone in his epic 1987 arm-wrestling movie *Over the Top*.

LAUGHINGSTOCK!

If I adopted a goat in Belize, I have just one question,
If I missed her so, would I get visitation rights?

If he suffered from Tennis Elbow and Swimmer's Ear,
Would he be worried about Athlete's Foot?

If I was funny and had the time, no question . . .
I would set up a comedy festival called Laughingstock!

By Yatter

Ahmed's belly rumbled. 'That'd be 22 hours, Elvis, we're doing well. No, you have to fast with me, only another two to go. Hey, stop whimpering, you've got plenty of water. Yeah, I know, I'm hungry too.' The pair of them were seriously famished, but Ahmed was determined, and his first ever fast was going well. But a hungry dog is not a happy dog, and a confused Elvis was whining constantly.

Ahmed had some shopping to do. He was scouring the small ads in the previous day's *Aldershot Herald:*

Wrapping paper, 10 sheets of brown parcel wrapping paper, unused, 70cm × 114 cm. Bargain at just £1. Telephone 375499

Wicker coffee table, shelf underneath, reasonable condition hence price only £15 ono, collection only. Also *Dulux* paintpod with extra reach handle, £35. Call 938933

Flip flops, navy, ladies, size 40/41, still with tags on, £3. Tel: 375029

Prism mobility scooter, one careful owner, £425 ono, call me on 626639

Pipe bender, professional A-frame, Hilmor CM35, superb condition, cost £600, asking £200. Bob 07700 900787

Loft ladder 2-section sliding aluminium, no bracket available, hence just £25. Tel 424390

Steve's Dog Walking and house sitting, registered, reliable and insured. 07715 674299

Arthur Sarnoff framed prints × 2, dogs playing pool, ideal gift Plus Rick Astley record 33rpm, £2.50. telephone 07742 482382

Foot spa and facial steamer, unwanted Xmas presents, mint, £15 each or £25 for both. 622753 evenings only

Sylvanian Families, large manor house, lodge and pieces of furniture. Great value £40. 637821, Beverly

Rucksack, medium size, durable, practical and comfortable, cost £45, will accept £12. Call Phillip 585923

This last ad caught Ahmed's eye, and he lent over Elvis to pick up the phone. 585923. 'Ugh . . . yes, hullo. My name is Ahm . . .' he corrected himself just in time, surely he should give himself a fake name, just in case? Come on Ahmed, you're not thinking!

'. . . Dimitri.' It was the first name that came to him – strange as he'd never met anyone with that name and couldn't think of one on TV or elsewhere. 'I'm ringing about the rucksack, I don't suppose it's still for sale, is it by any chance?'

A frail female emerged through the plastic grill by his ear after what seemed an eternity, betraying faint Yorkshire inflections, and speaking slowly. 'Well, Dimitri, I'm afraid you've called at a rather bad time. I'm sorry to say that my husband Phillip passed away in his sleep last night. I thought you might have been our son calling from Dubai. But still, you know, he would have wanted you to take the rucksack, I'm sure, you sound like a kind young man. I don't think he'll miss it now, will he?' The line went silent for a few seconds, but surely she didn't honestly want him to answer? 'Can you come and pick it up this afternoon? I'm on the Farnborough Road, just near Sunny Hill, we're not going anywhere today.'

Later that afternoon Ahmed and Elvis were strolling back home and had just passed the new Hair & Scalp Centre. Ahmed whistled as he adjusted the straps of his new purchase. Poor old Phillip had been right: the rucksack was indeed extremely comfortable. Ahmed knew that it was empty, but he could tell these things, and had been pleased to find all clasps, clips and fabric in a generally decent state of repair. The item had been a reasonable and successful purchase, so both parties involved in the deal had parted on good terms, completely satisfied. The bereaved lady had even gone as far as to mention the fact that Phillip would have been pleased with the trade, so the entire transaction had evidently been a resounding success. It also looked very durable and practical, as the late Phillip had again promised in the Classifieds. The deceased had clearly been a decent and honest man, thought Ahmed, wishing that they had had the opportunity to meet. He pondered briefly that their paths may have indeed crossed more than once . . . perhaps when silently waiting next to each other in a supermarket queue with goods in hand, or maybe Phillip had gestured in thanks as Ahmed let his rusting Nissan Micra out at the Sallow Down crossroads on the edge of town a few years previously . . . it's even possible that they'd shared fleeting eye contact while one of the men kindly held open the library door one afternoon to let the other pass. After all, modestly-sized Aldershot was not the metropolis to end all metropolises.

Ahmed/Peter/Dimitri had dwelled briefly on offering the grieving widow £10 instead of £12 (especially after noting on careful inspection that there was a disappointing coin-sized stain located on the greasy underside of the right-hand side pocket), but, given the circumstances, he begrudgingly paid her the full asking price without entering into any negotiation. It seemed to be just the right size for the home-made explosive device that he was going to construct; at least, it was roughly the dimensions, judging from the instructions he'd received in the morning's email from his mentor. He had also been instructed that the following day he was to meet an unnamed operative who would come to RonJoyce at midday. This mystery person would bring all the necessary materials and chemicals to make the bomb, and give further instructions.

Midday came and went with Ahmed apprehensively pacing about the living room, mumbling incoherently to Elvis. Having never experienced such hunger ever in his life, he surprised himself by feeling unusually alert and mentally aware, sharp as a tack. That pesky left eye flickered randomly, but became still just as suddenly as it had jerkily convulsed. The familiar RonJoyce doorbell rang, which prompted Elvis to bark once and jump off the sofa, dribbling saliva. Ahmed noticed from the time on *Sky News* that it was 12:42 p.m. 'Well, he may be late, but at least he's here', he said out loud as he went to get the door. *He* was in fact a *she*. 'Hi, I think you know why I'm here . . .' the girl offered, forcing a wry smile.

'Um, yes. Please come in, oh let me take that.' The girl, who couldn't have been much more than 20 years old, had a bulky suitcase with wheels that Ahmed dragged into the house and through to the living room, where the girl now stood. She seemed to be making a concerted effort not to look around or be nosy, but just to stand neutrally and explain her mission.

'I've brought everything that you'll need. Please, no names, we don't need to know anything about each other. All I know is that you have been chosen, and I am here to help. I am a foot soldier, ready to do *His Will*. Primer, detonator, containers, chemicals, wiring, all the instructions in detail . . . it's all in the suitcase, which you could burn in your garden at some point soon, couldn't you? Enjoy the wedding. So I'll be off then, no questions, no?' It was delivered more as a statement than a question, it was clear that she didn't want to hang around. Ahmed was a bit taken aback. *Wedding?* This must be some sort of code, he figured. He was at first surprised to find a girl at the door, especially one so pretty and young, and it had put him a little on the back foot. He thought that she was probably Asian, although he really couldn't be sure, and she chose not to wear a headscarf, instead allowing glorious shiny black hair to tumble over her shoulders. With an unwavering voice that displayed little emotion she was efficient and well-spoken, giving off the confident air of somebody who had been well brought up and well educated. Her youthful face and apparent innocence belied a darker belief inside, complicit in Ahmed's evil intentions. The brevity of the visit also confused him somewhat, but he just about managed an awkward 'No, uh, no questions, I suppose' in reply as she left in a flash, as suddenly as she had appeared.

Ahmed felt deflated once again, a familiar emotion to him. It was his first encounter with a like-minded crusader, and it wasn't meant to have been like this. Some morale-boosting camaraderie with a couple of lads, talking about the struggle, different clerics, the evil in the West, potential targets . . . that is what he would have liked, not this perfunctory and unsatisfying exchange. Nevertheless, his spirits lifted a little as he slowly unzipped the suitcase on the highly polished dark wood dining table, an heirloom from his parents (along with the vast majority of the furniture in the house). The first thing that hit him was the strong mustiness coming from inside: it was the bag itself that stank, nothing to do with its contents. A waft of old man blended with an undercurrent of dank cave and even perhaps a tinge of moss, subtle hints of peat bog overshadowing a solid bedrock pong of well-used running shoes, while a faint shade of petrol added distinct piquancy, all combined with a slight yet discernible nose of blackcurrant. He wondered where Girl A had acquired it. From her Grandfather's wardrobe, perhaps, or did she pick it up in Oxfam last week for £1.50? Maybe she'd been handed it with everything already inside, and it's very possible she may not even have looked in it. He was never to know, so consciously stopped wondering and pulled the top back. 'Ahhh, Elvis, Elvis . . . this is really a green-light situation we have here, dog. A green-light situation.'

A little while later, Elvis gobbled up his delicious Quality Beef and Country Vegetable Moist and Meaty Chunks. Packed with vitamins, minerals, protein and carbohydrates to help maintain good body condition, healthy teeth and strong bones, the meal was guaranteed by the manufacturer to provide a balanced source of nutrition and energy. Item Reference Number 597243 at Aldershot's leading purveyor of all your animal's needs – Purefoy's Dog Essentials, Est. 1989 – smelt foul. The substance contained in fact less than 4% meat or *animal derivatives*, the nastiest and roughest cuts that even the most carnivorous human would discard. Masquerading as food it consisted primarily of cereals which bulked it out cheaply, with an assortment of unpronounceable colourants, antioxidants, preservatives and other additives accounting for no less than twelve E Numbers. Despite all this, the frantic dog didn't even come up for air until the bowl had been licked clean. Ahmed hauled the 25kg sack of canine biscuit chunks back to its storage place under the sink. He noticed that the bag clearly stated on the back: *this bag is not a toy. To avoid risk of suffocation keep out of reach of children and pets.* Ahmed therefore made sure that the door to the cupboard was firmly closed, having had his responsibilities to the animal in terms of safety made very clear. Elvis slobbered water around, some actually reaching the interior of his mouth cavity, before shaking his body violently as if performing some sort of ritualistic dance of satisfaction. Ahmed's belly, on the other hand, felt like a void. His imagined his stomach imploding, twisting and gurgling before digesting itself in its own acid. Could this destructive liquid then burn down inside him through glutinous tissue, destroying everything in its path (perhaps missing vital organs, at least?) before juice angrily froths out of a hole in his groin or the upper leg area? He decided to eat. Elvis's ravenous master attacked the defensive packaging of the dates as he sat on the sofa in front of *Sky News* with the heavily made-up Julia Downing. Elvis jumped up clumsily to settle in. Julia was his favourite, and he liked the colour of her lipstick, an unsubtle but effective hooker red. He would sometimes stare at her, even with the sound muted, and let his mind drift.

'. . . it was the Israeli submarine, the *Tannin*, a third of whose 466 million pound cost was incidentally paid for by the German government as part of war reparations from decades ago, which reports coming in suggest was the aggressor on this occasion . . .' the TV informed him.

Ahmed stuffed the first three dates into his mouth in quick succession, paused, then hurriedly dispatched the rest of the box. Sticky morsels clung to his now bushy beard just under his bottom lip as the pile of stones grew in the date-box lid. On returning to the kitchen as the weather forecast came on, he clicked on the electric kettle for a coffee, and leant up to reach an oblong tin of sardines from the top of the neat pile in the cupboard above the toaster. Gingerly prising back the razor-sharp metal, he carefully curled the potential weapon upwards as the fishy niff invaded his nostrils. 'Not this time, oh vicious tin,' Ahmed spoke out loud, checking on the scar tissue that crossed the palm of his hand, which sometimes made him feel like some kind of Action Hero from the world of Hollywood. Now he considered his role in real life, as it dawned on him that events in the not-too-distant future could easily transfer to the big screen, dramatic as they were surely to be . . .

Be
Live
Discover
Forage
Consider
Process
Formulate
Cultivate
Enjoy
Originate
Relax
Ruminate
Meditate
Persist
Act

Sue's list had been expanding daily, and she was now satisfied with her bullet points for life/work/action. The words were to be printed and placed on the walls all around her office, the aim being to serve as a constant reminder of her intentions, as well as encouragement and inspiration to hand. Everyone needs a good list, she had told herself, otherwise the world would grind to a disorganised halt. She had re-invented herself as a Self-Development Guru, and her plan was to pen a series of self-help books for women. While using her life experience to inject pearls of wisdom into each publication (that she would get printed up herself), there would be the opportunity to sell the books at self-help seminars (which she would also set up and promote), and, of course, online. Each book basically had the same vapid message, bulkily padded out with over-worded waffle to bring the paperback up to an acceptable size and weight, ready to persuade the weaker of the fairer sex to part with their hard-earned cash (or that of their husbands). The covers were to be eye-catching, female-friendly and inoffensive, and the books were to retail at a perfectly reasonable £7.99. She had just finished *Time Management for the Worried Working Mum*, and was delighted with the cover, which featured a 30-something-year-old plain-looking brunette frowning up at an oversized antique station clock (a flash of an idea that had come to her out of nowhere while in the shower one morning). Sue couldn't quite decide if next she should start *Confidence Starts in the Womb* or *Miserable Menopause? I Don't Think So . . . !* After considering, processing and eventually cultivating her thoughts, she had decided on a course of action. She would spend mornings on *Confidence*, which would leave afternoons to concentrate on *Menopause*, thereby allowing several hours in the evening to spend time with Claude, plus a break for lunch at some point. This precisely-organised scheduling was devised as a direct result of the hours considering and documenting the *Time Management* book, advice and schemes dreamt up by her (the self-proclaimed *expert*) over the last few months for the now-finished latest oeuvre. So now she followed her own teachings, found . . . for reader's reference . . . in Chapter 3, Part 2 (iv) of *Time Management for the Worried Working Mum:*

> *'If you ever find yourself at a crossroads as we all do at various periods in our complicated lives, unable to make that decision about which road to take, it is always preferable to leave your options open and to try to keep juggling everything equally until the path becomes clear. Compartmentalise, ensuring that you divide your time and efforts as fairly as the day's hours permit, and you will soon discover a balance and harmony will fill your being, existence and spirit.'*

Sue had followed her own teaching, and it appeared to be working out. This gave her more confidence in herself and her abilities, which in itself was a great help and put her in exactly the right frame of mind as she started the notes and structure map for *Confidence Starts in the Womb.* Since she had left Tom and started her new life with Claude she had undergone a change within that shocked even herself when she considered it. An immense self-assertiveness had swept over her which brought alongside it a previously untapped fortitude to her character, and it was this tidal wave of self-belief that had given her the inspiration to become an overnight Self-Help Expert. Various titles were neatly listed in her notebook as possible future projects, including:

Ditch that Man, You Can Rise Above Him (and make all men Want You).

You Don't have to be Mean to Live within your Means: the Money Guide for Ladies that Lunch.

Help with Your Life: Life Points to Succeed and Win at Life!

Inside Supermarket Shopping: how to spot Deals and Buy well for your Family.

There is only One Self-Help book, and you're Looking at it!

Banish Anxiety and Emotional Stress within Hours of Reading the Last Page of this Book.

Healing and Self-Worth Part I.

Healing and Self-Worth Part II.

The Journey from the Soul, and What Lies Beyond.

199 Ways to Influence People and Win at Life.

The Empowered Female.

Delete Depression in Days, Definitely!

On Being a Jewish Feminist: a Guide for the over 60s.

Raising Happy Children.

Relationship Re-generation Guide (We're on the Same Page. It's an Empty page, but it's the Same Page).

The Key to Handling Stress and Depression, plus How to take Charge of your own Destiny while Maintaining Strong Relationships and a Healthy Bank Balance, Cheering Others up and Giving up Negative Thoughts: a Guide.

Her self-editing policy was often irrelevant (if in fact it existed at all), and dreaming up punchy titles sometimes evidently remained beyond her reach. Large amounts of waffle remained the key factor here, whether in the title or the content. Claude was bemused with Sue's dedication and drive, and didn't really understand what it was all about. He would leave her to it, observing from the sidelines without much comprehension of what she was up to, but was quietly supportive and would offer encouraging noises at all the right moments. Clearly his new lover was not the kind of woman who would let the grass grow under her feet. Her recently purchased bonsai tree, however, was tended to with extreme care. Sue would gently caress the leaves with her words, talking at length to the mini tree after its daily tending, carried out with the utmost respect (and her red mini watering-can, straight out of *Snow White & the Seven Dwarves*). This was all part of her new regime, new routine, new life. She worked constantly, churning out the words, tapping away at the keyboard or carefully précising thoughts with a well-chewed pencil. She used a white Apple Mac laptop microcomputer running the latest edition of Word, and had bought a number of expensive notebooks and assorted stationery items. Her theory was that if she was jotting down an idea, it would make her feel like she's writing something important if it were written in a top-of-the-range quality notepad, and that made her feel good.

Sue even had another side-project in the wings, but it

was currently on the back-burner until the time was right. She also intended to muscle her way in with supermarkets or cosmetics companies and the like, aspiring to be the person who dreams up the descriptions for products, especially bathroom or beauty items. She could imagine her writing style sitting comfortably on certain tubes or bottles, and had started making notes:

Gently squeeze a small amount of product onto the palm of your hand and enjoy rubbing it into a foam with a little warm water. Rub your face, luxuriate in the great textures and delicate scent whilst taking care to avoid the area of the eyes. Take a deep breath, rinse and pat dry. OR

Let the conditioner nourish the very life of your hair, from follicle to tip. Natural shine, spring and vitality will be restored, especially with regular applications (at least once a week is recommended). OR EVEN

Apply WartAway® carefully to the skin once a day for up to two weeks, taking care not to damage good skin around the offending wart. Results should be seen after a few days, and excess skin can be sloughed away by a pumice stone, using a circular motion. If problem persists, consult your doctor.

Food and drink descriptions would come easily and quickly, she was sure.

Kwamini © Tea is harvested with care, and only the finest tips are selected by hand. This Fairtrade organic crop grows in the middle of a nature reserve high in the Chinese tea plantations, where Souchong's large leaves are smoked in the traditional way. Brew for a few minutes to release the characteristic orange-tinged hue in this magnificent slightly spiced beverage, often enjoyed to accompany savoury food.

OR

McCraig's Sabres © are deliciously crunchy biscuits, generously coated with a layer of smooth chocolate. Rich in cereals, they provide a decent amount of your daily fibre requirements as well as helping with a healthy nutritional intake whilst pleasuring your palette to the utmost!

From time to time, however, she would take mini-breaks from her work, often to spend a bit of time on Facebook. She loved to post hilariously poignant life anecdotes, like:

> *I must have been half asleep this morning, I found that I'd put the box of Corn Flakes in the fridge door!!*
>
> *Isn't it annoying when you get shampoo in your eye?!*
>
> *Not happy with the man who stole my parking space at the supermarket this afternoon. I was about to reverse and there he was suddenly . . . he cut me up and shot in, no shame!!*

Recently a hypnotherapist friend had turned her onto a brand of herbal tea called Celestial ™ that she would constantly sip scolding mugs of throughout the day. The colourful label, clearly inspired by classical Indian art, promised '*an aromatic, joyful and uplifting experience that will infuse the soul, revealing your inner senses whilst celebrating the very essence of life itself.*' It appeared to be working, and working well . . . or so Sue believed. And if she believed it, then it *was* working.

The masterplan was also to translate into various languages

with the aim of taking the products truly global, and so preliminary discussions had already started with an officially-registered French translator, who happened to be her doctor's wife. She sometimes imagined that in a few years she would be jetting around the world in First Class, giving seminars and attending conferences as guest speaker. All of this brand-new start would require a new wardrobe at some juncture, with power-dressing being key: the aim was to ensure a professional look whilst retaining her femininity, but perhaps occasionally hinting at sexiness, depending on the occasion. The clothes needed to be expensive but not flashy, smart without being too formal, impressive but not daunting, and neither too flamboyant nor frumpy. She decided to go on a bit of a shopping spree in the UK on her next trip over. Sue's hippy credentials at the forefront of her writing, an unswerving self-belief in her business acumen, a hungry and gullible mass audience ready to flex their credit cards, were all positive factors that would ensure a great future for the set-up. The icing on the cake came after she purchased a Doctorate online from a 'university' based in Fuengirola, Spain for €495, using a new surname, so 28 days later her *nom de plume* became Dr. Susan T. Soloman. She considered the name to hold a certain authoritative weight, which would impress potential purchasers. At least it had a ring to it . . . more so than a plain and forgettable Sue Collins. The certificate was framed and proudly displayed on the wall of her office, and she had no problem assuming the role of her alter ego as she sat down at her desk every morning. Dr. Susan T. Soloman was at work.

Polly lounged on the floor cushions piled up towards the corner of the living room. She was back with Brian at the

Welsh retreat for spiritual enlightenment and well-being, but as yet was still to feel the vibes that should bring about the desired frame of mind. Unfortunately, she was still mad with her father, Tony, after his ultimatum regarding Brian who she regarded as the love of her life. This anger was directly at odds with Brian's doctrines, so she had not mentioned anything about it to him, but it weighed on her mind a lot of the time. Did her dad really expect her to settle down with a banker or lawyer? How could anyone not love this gentle, resourceful leader of men who is Brian?

The stone cottage had been a lucky find, especially as Brian had agreed very favourable terms with the landlord. The negotiations hadn't always been plain sailing as the local man's thick accent was a barrier for a while, but with lots of repetition, a pen and pad of paper, plus the services of a costly lawyer, they had arrived at some middle ground and sealed the deal. The property was suitably remote, a fairly spacious barn room was attached, ideal for meetings and discussion groups.

Polly was proud of Brian's achievements and focus, and she could see how the others respected him, listening attentively to his lectures and viewpoints, digesting and supporting. The group had grown even in the last few weeks, and there was a regular core of about thirty followers. It had reached the point that Brian had decided to set up as some kind of official unit, and it was time to decide on a suitable name. 'How about Equinox?' Polly suggested.

Brian stopped chopping carrots and half-turned. 'Hhhmm, not bad. Not bad. But maybe it's a bit . . . well, geographical-sounding. Not sure, but I was considering The Onward Soldiers.'

'Yep, it's okay, but it kinda reminds me of The Salvation

Army!' laughed Polly. 'I've got a goodun' for you, B. The Brian-tologists!'

Brian frowned. Then, unusually, he raised his voice. 'Look, Polly, if you're not going to take this seriously . . . this isn't a joke, you know. And we're nothing like that lot.' He was abrupt, and starting dicing veg again, quicker than before.

'Ok, okay. Sorry honey, I was just messing around. Can I give you a hand with the soup?'

Brian was preparing a huge cauldron of vegetable broth for the evening's meeting; it was to be an offering to the assembled friends. He had vague plans to plough up the lawn behind the cottage, to grow their own vegetables for the group, and perhaps build a shed for some goats. His followers had promised not to eat all day in order to purge their bodies and become mentally sharp to discuss their progress, as well as plans for the organization. He intended to present them with the group's name in a few hours, but he still hadn't decided on what to call it. A few names were in the hat: Parallelism, The Genesis Faction, 41 Days 41 Nights, and The Nemesis Throne.

'No, I can manage. You rest.' Then Brian dramatically swung round from the chopping board by the sink, a broad grin pouring through his beard. 'I've got it. I've got the name, it's been sent and I have received it. This is perfect. We are going to call ourselves . . . wait for it . . . THE SECTION.'

And so it came to pass, that evening, when the tribe was assembled, a barefooted Brian gave a rousing quasi-religious speech, his eyes often moist with emotion, an ecstatic expression across his face. 'We are the chosen ones who will surpass the human of today, we are years ahead, and with that knowledge we are nearer our salvation. *They* are stuck in their image of today . . . an evil rat race of TV, internet, banking and immoral conduct is what drives them in their grim lives. Together we will shun these horrors, combining resources and strength to become a force for good, a lifeline for each other, collectively pooling our knowledge to further the cause. We will work shoulder to shoulder, working up through the ranks, and I urge you to distance yourselves from those who refuse to listen and open their hearts to the way of truth. We shall grow in numbers, and our voice will be heard around all the corners of the world. More humans will become an integral part of our organisation, multiplying, spreading its power and helping the people along their lifelong journey towards spiritual freedom and happiness. Forget the lost souls, the negative emotions which are all around outside of these walls. Inside, together we are safe and strong as one unit, one family, one matrix of thought with forward-looking ideas and philosophies. We refuse to stand still, but instead will not miss the large signpost up ahead, the signpost which says HAPPINESS .

'Working between us and for ourselves, we can improve and rehabilitate our lives and those of our fellow believers by our side. It may be hard to leave friends or even family on the other side, but you know deep in your hearts that they will follow if they want to walk the path with us. You will miss TV, radio and internet, but not for long. We do not need their negative forces polluting our beautiful union. It is the moment to revise our lives, and climb the Scale of Awareness, a concept that I have been developing which I will explain to you all in good time. For now, though, we must not run before we can walk. Your patience will be dutifully rewarded. Being fortunate enough to be part of this historic birth of our group of friends is in fact not a choice, it was always intended this way. . . ' He paused for effect, dramatically lifting his forearm to wipe beads of sweat from his brow. Standing triumphantly, back straight, he very deliberately delivered the line that he had been honing to perfection in front of the bedroom mirror an hour previously. 'We now have a name, a focus, an identity. I am delighted to include you, my friends, in this exciting and exclusive band of like-minded good people, at the birth of my project – now *our* project, which is now a reality. Our group is now called . . . THE SECTION.'

The tribe burst in applause and joyful laughter, as dyed-in-the-wool members of The Section hugged each other; there were even a few tears. The realisation dawned on Brian that he had achieved his first goal, clearing the first hurdle with ease. He now had these people eating out of the palm of his hand, he had a new premises, and a good woman at his side whose dedication and love was absolute. The second phase would soon have to be initiated, in which the extraction of funds from the members of The Section was to begin. But first, he would have to dedicate more time gaining people's trust and respect, which would involve more action and words until they would do almost anything for him and the tribe.

'And now, friends, we must take time to wash our feet, the cleansing process that will purge our souls and prepare us on the right track for our work. After this, we will feast on soup, before meditation.'

Polly fetched a few washing-up bowls and towels from the cottage, and some of the followers helped to fill them with warm water. Small groups naturally formed around the room, and the feet-washing started. The babble of animated conversation echoed around the barn as shoes and socks were removed and the joyful procedure was carried out. Brian mingled around the people, offering praise and encouragement, yet maintaining a strictly not-too-personal air about him, which he felt was becoming to his leader status. Before long, Polly was on her knees, sponging Brian's feet, before drying them with a tea towel . . . an act that reminded them both of the evening of their first encounter when she had done pretty much the same at the flat back in Clapham. He smiled down serenely at her, in silence. The air around them was charged with optimism, the room buzzing, everyone present believing that they were at the birth of something truly amazing and life-altering.

On opening her car door, a waft of cigarette smoke hit Sue as it so often did when out and about in France, reminding her vividly of her previous 20-a-day habit, which felt like a lifetime ago. It had been a few years since she'd quit cold turkey; she had found it remarkably easy, even with the bouts of terrible insomnia that were followed by rather odd recurring dreams. A giant polystyrene cigarette would majestically yet somehow clumsily float through the red sky like an enormous Pink Floyd-esque Zeppelin, bobbing around before flying into a cloud of smoke. This went on for days, and she would always have a sharp and focused memory of it upon waking. The images became more sporadic over weeks until finally the dreams stopped. But for all of the bad press that smoking attracted in the UK, it still seemed to be a national sport in France, more noticeably so when you were an ex-smoker. From 13-year-olds furtively chuffing their precious shared fags blowing smoke rings at each other, to the 87-year-old Great Grandmother chugging determinedly on her lifetime's 432,291st cancer stick yet remaining miraculously cancer- and death-free, it seemed as if all walks of life were having a go. It was, however, a more unpleasant odour that greeted Sue on her arrival at the supermarket. Whiffs of sweat, not fully disguised by bleach, invaded her nostrils as automatic doors clumsily parted. A minute passed . . . her brain negated the smell, which ceased to bother her. 'Life is all about small victories,' she considered smugly, pleased with herself for having found the nearest parking space to the shop's entrance (that wasn't a disabled or a mother/baby space, of course). She negotiated past a spotty and awkward teenager with longish hair who was gormlessly meandering about, clasping a two-litre bottle of Coke as if it was an extension of his body. A tall figure sidled past, gingerly cradling a couple of bags of ices cubes. Not being a warm day, Sue surmised that: a) there was a party going on that she hadn't been invited to, or b) someone had broken their arm or twisted a limb, resulting in a dolorous soft-tissue injury that required ice application. Sue found herself gorping into the deep-chiller unit which was taking up most of the aisle in the local LeClerc supermarket meat section. It was stinking slightly, if that's possible, and it was probably this stench that aroused her interest during her nonchalant afternoon stroll about. Behind her she could hear the efforts of a ruddy over-sized vendor calling out sporadically in his attempts to entice shoppers to sample and hopefully purchase certain meat-based products. Suddenly she recoiled, bolt upright whilst scrunching both mouth and nose up in disgust. Daring to peer back down again to the depths of the cavernous fridge she confirmed to herself that there were indeed nearly ten complete pig's heads sitting quietly at the bottom of the chiller, chilling. As there was nothing else in the fridge, the macabre exhibition could easily have been a Damien Hirst installation with a million-dollar price tag. All of her attention was momentarily directed at these heads, and she couldn't prise her scrutiny away from them. Large snouts were pressing into the polythene covering as the ears somehow found their own squashed space, eyes mercifully closed under impressive damp lashes. Greasy, barcoded price stickers had been placed somewhere over the cheek area on each tightly wrapped package of flesh – but they barely managed to stick due to the presence of unknown juices – and Sue was too transfixed, horrified and shocked to lean down to check the price of a pig's head, despite a shopper's curiosity that wanted to know. A humourless-looking woman of indeterminate age, perhaps late 50s, appeared at her shoulder, bringing Sue back to normal supermarket life. Sue noticed her boyish haircut, round glasses and ill-fitting black jeans. She enjoyed sensible shoes and wore a hiking jacket over her sensible jumper, but nothing would disguise her soft, regular yet dangerous-sounding cough. As she leant down to hoik out one of the more sizeable heads, Sue felt sick. The woman waddled off past the halal meats, still muttering, prize in hand. A few thoughts sprang to mind:

'I am glad to have been born a human.'

'Has anyone around here read *The Lord of the Flies?*'

'What is that lady going to cook later – fried ears, broiled cheek?'

Sue hurried away to the relative safety of the cheese, butter and yoghurt area; the sight of a thousand cheeses made her feel a little better, and by the time she arrived in the booze aisle her worries had evaporated. There, right there in all his glory, stood Keith. The first thing that struck Sue was how ridiculous he appeared in his Ferrari baseball cap: a man of his age in rural France, it just looked absurd.

'Oh, Sue,' he almost stuttered. 'How's you?'

'Keith – well, very well thanks. Yes, very well,' she reassured herself. 'How's things with you?'

'Well, you know, keeping busy. I just posted off my parking ticket fine from the other day. €12, that's all the fine was . . . I nearly wrote a bloody thank-you note with the cheque! Would've been 90 quid in the UK. I mowed the lawn all day yesterday, so I thought I'd better get out and about a bit today, hence this little bit of light shopping,' he explained. Sue chuckled inwardly. Every single time she saw Keith he seemed to justify himself with tales of domestic life or manly work around the house, and it always involved mowing *that* lawn. The grass should be an immaculate prize-winner judging by the amount of time that he claimed to spend tending to it, but she knew that it was in reality a scrappy field around the back of his unkempt house. It had been several weeks since she had left Tom, and she hadn't seen or heard from him. There was a part of her that wanted to know what kind of state he was in, and she didn't want to hang about.

'And have you seen Tom recently?'

'Yeah, all's fine. Tom has been, well . . . how should I say? He's been caning the drink, you know, I don't think he's taken it too well.'

He detected a look of concern flash across Sue's face. 'Well, to be honest, Sue, he's gay these days and keeps suggesting that we *do something . . .*'

Sue looked momentarily horrified.

'God, look at your face . . . I'm only messing with you, Sue! He's okay, just boozing a bit hard, you know. He's even got one of those beer chiller dispenser things so he can have decent draught lager at home, he's as chuffed as mint balls with it. Listen, here's my email address, just drop me a message and I'll keep you updated if you want.' He gave her a card from his wallet. Sue thought that it was all a bit odd, but she took it anyway. Even if she couldn't admit it to herself, she was still interested in Tom, and although she certainly didn't want to actually see him, she could still find out about him, which was perfect. She left Keith squinting at the labels on endless bottles of whisky, trying to decide between the two cheapest available. He ended up buying both, the alcoholic's most sensible option. After gathering her thoughts, she joined a queue at checkout number six, where an odd-looking local girl with a moon-like face into which small black eyes were sunken was grappling with the till. The use of cheque books in this day and age in France still surprised her and the majority of the older generation always paid this way, often causing tailbacks at supermarket checkouts. At the till and taking forever was a woman who bore a remarkable resemblance to Brian May from Queen, yabbering away with cheque book in hand, oblivious to the queue forming behind her. It was when Sue eventually reached the invigorating freshness of outside nine long minutes later that she sensed an urgent and brisk tightening of the air. In an instant the town darkened, as if at once plunged from brilliant sunshine into shade. The wind picked up, clouds streaming across the fractured sky as the rain started to fall. It was not normal rain. Random, sparse and huge drops came down, almost hurting as they spattered her face and hands. It felt warm, the water, and Sue suddenly realised that she needed a wash. She would wash away the memory of the pig's heads and have a long soak in the bathtub when she got home. It was not a normal day.

Norman leant over the edge of the stained sofa, muting inane daytime TV with one hand while hoping to pick up the phone with the other before it abused him again with its violent electronic cry (a grey Panasonic AU-90, now discontinued, ringtone selected: 'Wake Alert Classic').

'It's Polly . . . it's me . . . sis. You all right?'

'Hiya Polls. Yeah, all good here. In fact, all great here!' Norm replied.

'You're not stoned again, are you, Norm? It's only lunchtime!'

'Nah, of course not.'

He had, in fact, just put out his third spliff of the day after getting out of bed with a slight Jamaican hangover at 11 a.m., and the day was floating along gently. He wasn't going to let on that he'd been on a *wake and bake* programme for years now. 'I'm all booked for the jolly to India. It's two weeks on the beach, a final party, loads of drugs and loads of sunburn. *Then* I'm going to be sensible and grow up. I think Dad's got a point, and I'm really gonna try to straighten out. I'm a fully-grown man and I need to sort myself out. But I'm not going to be too dull, first . . . party! I'm off next Sunday, can't wait. What's new? What's going on with Brian, then? You seen him recently?' he enquired.

He knew full well that Polly wouldn't have given in to their father Tony's blackmail – she had always been far too headstrong for that.

'Of course I have. For all I care, Dad can give all his stinking money to the Ilfracombe Library or The Woking Cat Sanctuary – if such places exist! That's great about India, you'll have a great time. I'd love to come over, but I'm busy with things, lots going on with me at the mo. You know . . . well, Brian's set up this group, and he has . . . well, *followers.*

I'm at his side and we've kind of done it together, it's great. I've never felt like this before, about anything really. He has incredible vision, with these great ideas and philosophies that people need to hear. He cares for . . .'

'You what?' Norman interrupted. 'Don't tell me it's a bloody cult or something? It certainly sounds like it.'

'No, of course not!' Polly retorted defensively, a little too quickly, Norman noticed. At that moment Yatter entered the living room. He didn't seem to care that Norman was clearly busy on the phone.

'It's ED!' said Yatter to the room, with a smile.

'Who's ED?' replied Norman instinctively.

'What are you talking about? Who's ED?' came the bemused voice down the phone line.

Yatter was on a roll. 'E is for Electric. D for Dwarf. I can't believe I've never spotted it before, ED. Or do you prefer Edward?' He watched Norman (now christened Edward, the Electric Dwarf or ED) squirm with annoyance. He had also deliberately spoken loudly, so whoever was on the phone would hear, even though he had no clue who it was.

Norman gave him the finger. 'Look, I'm on the phone, okay?' he snapped. 'You're not funny anyway.'

'Sorry, Poll, don't worry about it, it's just Yatter messing around.'

But Polly had heard it all. 'Don't let that arsehole be so out of order with you. He's a bully. You should come and speak to Brian and . . .'

'Look, sis. This group, what the hell's it all about? It sounds weird.'

There was a slight pause. Yatter was still hovering about, smirking. Norman knew that he'd put Polly on the spot. She explained, and Norman could sense that she was being careful with her words. 'We are called The Section. We're growing in number, maybe up to around eighty now, evolving into one large family. It's not a religious thing, but we have great ideas and a companionship that is like nothing else I've ever experienced. We don't need money, so everyone is encouraged to come and live at the retreat and to give their funds to Brian and the group. We like to be free with ourselves and the expression of our . . .'

'It's a fucking cult, a cult I'm telling you! What the hell are you doing? The guy's a nutter and a conman! You can't . . .' Norman tailed off, a bit too stoned to explain himself coherently.

'Norman,' said Polly coldly. 'Don't speak about Brian that way, take the cork out of your arse, and if you won't listen I won't bother telling you.' And she hung up the phone. Neither of them were to know that it was to be the last time that they would ever speak to each other.

Yatter was laughing by the kitchen. 'Edward's sister's in a cult, Edward's sister's in a cult. Da de da de da de da, da de da de da de da,' he chanted. 'Edward's sister's in a cult, da de da de . . .'

Norman turned to face Yatter and shouted, surprising even himself, 'FUCK OFF YOU PRICK!'

Yatter sheepishly retreated into his room and sat on his bed to make an entry in his book, *The Bad Poet's Society.* It had been swirling around in his mind recently, and he just *had* to jot this down.

THE GIFT OF THE CENTURY

If you offer a peppermill without peppercorns
It's as irritating as offering a child a remote-controlled toy
At Christmastime . . .
Without batteries.

By Yatter

In Wales, Polly was shaking. She too had surprised herself with her solid defence of The Section and the argument with Norman. She was sitting alone on a wicker chair by the phone in the hallway for a while when Brian's hand landed on her skinny shoulder. 'Everything okay?' he enquired blandly.

'Sure,' she reassured him, 'it's all good.'

'Well, that's great. We're going to ramp it up tonight at the meet, you'll see, it'll be something.' He smiled, but without pleasure.

When Polly probed him inquisitively with moist eyes, he just repeated 'You'll see, you'll see.'

That evening the usual group was assembled in the barn, now just short of forty men and women. The atmosphere felt charged somehow, a little strained, possibly due to the sight of a sheep tethered to a stone weight next to a table on which sat a car battery, some jump leads, an ancient apothecary's glass bottle, an old book and a hunting knife. The excited yet muted chatter babbled past the beams overhead and reverberated around the eves. Everyone, including Polly, was waiting for the arrival of Brian, and Brian knew that everyone was expecting him at any time. That was why he delayed his arrival, in true star style, to whet the appetite of the followers until they were desperate. The newly-installed Bose Professional PA system eventually crackled into life, with Brian's instantly recognizable voice blasting out: 'Friends, followers, people of The Section . . . I love you.' This roused everyone to cheers, and everyone in the room was clapping and smiling as Brian bounded in, wireless microphone attached around his head, bobbing in front of his lips. He was clearly relishing his role, and moved like a svelte rock singer onstage at Madison Square Gardens. 'Yes, people, yes! I'm feeling the love, the good vibes, the positivity. This is why we are The Section . . . banishing the horrors which lie beyond the confines of this place, *our* beautiful place. Have we all washed our feet? Yes? That's great, the wonderful togetherness I'm feeling in this room . . . how we all watch each other's backs and look out for one another. We will not follow some ancient creed – as centuries of conflict and misery only go to prove to us beyond doubt that it doesn't work – we will trailblaze along our given path. It is us who will show the way, of which we alone can control the destiny.'

At this, Brian picked up a battered hardback copy of the King James Bible, and ripped out a couple of random pages. Without scrunching them or tearing them up, he smashed them into his dry mouth and grimaced as he chewed on the ageing paper and its bitter-tasting ink, before grabbing a small bottle of Evian from a back pocket, theatrically swilling the hideous mixture and tilting his head back to force it down his neck.

'Books like this Bible are of no interest on the inside, we have no need for irrelevant words among us. You are a beautiful family, *my* cherished family, and so I wish to share my recent vision with you.' He paused for effect, straightened up and continued to address the group, appearing to deliver his words to a non-existent listener at the back of the barn. 'Just last night, I had a dream in which the Spirit told me clearly that today, July 22nd, is The Section's *Sacred Date*. This will be our date every year, to be known simply as the Sacred Date. And on this date, we will sacrifice a sheep. This blessed animal will then be hung for a night, before being prepared for our tribe's feast tomorrow evening. In the Gospel according to St.Mark, Chapter 16, Verse 18, it is stated: *They will take up serpents, and if they drink anything deadly, it will by no means hurt them*. Does this have any significance for us and The Section? But of course, it all makes a lot of sense. So, to this end, and for the love of *our* God, I will now drink poison.' Brian suddenly picked up the bottle from the table, lifted the glass lid and, pushing his microphone down with the bottle, took three of four gulps of clear liquid. Looks of astonishment and panic filled the crowd, and fearful cries of 'No!' and 'Brian, what are you doing?' filled the barn. Polly rushed up to a smiling Brian, who dramatically wiped his mouth. 'We have nothing to fear, for God is on our side. Sometimes, especially as a Leader, we must demonstrate our Faith, even if maybe my life insurance doesn't stretch to this!' These words and the feeble quip reassured the followers and restored calm, but not for long, as Brian was now untangling the red and black jump leads. 'Here we have a 12-volt car battery, live and fully charged. The leads are attached, and it's all ready. I will first take the shock myself as an empathetic act of togetherness with the sheep.'

And so, before an astonished Polly could do anything to stop him, Brian efficiently clipped the crocodile clips onto his hands, before emitting a bizarrely gurgled and muted squeal as his body convulsed and jumped violently upwards and backwards before crashing down onto the hard ground. What joy Brian harboured in his heart, sensing an imminent burst of power over people! The harsh clamps had pulled the flesh clean off the backs of his burnt hands, and he lay curled up, bleeding and giving off a terrible stench which assailed his nostrils. A stunned silence was broken by Brian himself, who shouted out, 'THE SECTION !' Fortunately his headset was still in place despite the shock and fall, and his pained cry filled the barn and echoed beyond, bouncing around the courtyard between the farm buildings which hugged the side of a hill and clung together to form this unlikely settlement. One of the latest recruits, an older man called Derek, ran across to help Brian to his feet. He stood up, beaming and flashing his recently-whitened teeth to his followers as the entire room jumped up and applauded and shouted out. Brian knew that he had everyone glued to the spectacle, and he had absolute control. 'God gives us strength against the forked tongues, the evil world beyond these walls, and the greed of money that ravages mankind. We need nothing . . . not like those outside, yet we will want for nothing. Togetherness is the key, to be as one in an impenetrable circle of faith and harmony, here on this farm where we will support one another. If any of you wish to see me to discuss the liberation of worldly goods, please speak to me after.'

Without another word, Brian turned and swiftly picked up the knife, lunged at the top of the unwitting sheep's neck and stabbed wildly and with extraordinary aggression three times until the animal tottered over silently on its right side, crimson liquid spewing hideously from the fatal wounds. He walked slowly and exited the building, staring ahead and dripping blood as he left. Silence filled the air, and the group was left stunned by the sequence of events it had just witnessed, which were like a *Carry On* movie directed by David Cronenberg. The pretty and young Jordan towards the back of the crowd surprised herself by enjoying an intense attack of lechery for Brian. She smiled for the first time that day, brimming with desire.

Brian had, in fact, managed to liberate large amounts of cash from fourteen members of The Section, even a detached house in Bristol, and had amassed significant personal wealth from the ongoing operation. This he had divulged to Polly, but only a much watered-down version of the magnitude of his successes, letting her believe that it was all for the advancement of the group. The Cayman Islands Trust operation that he had set up with a cunning financial advisor remained his little secret, as did the modest £150,000 that he had recently set aside in his personal current account for spending money. He was wise, however, and had never flashed the cash, preferring to hoard it away for the most part now, waiting for the day when he could decide that enough was enough.

Elvis was sniffing gingerly around the suitcase that lay open by the TV, laying bare its deadly contents in kit form. Meanwhile Ahmed sat on the edge of the sofa with an instant coffee, uninjured hand perched slightly over the rim of the mug as he savoured the sensation of hot wet steam on his palm and fingers. There was no particular sound in the house, just that of the dog doing his thing, scrabbling about, perplexed at the unfamiliar item and its strange scents. Ahmed felt a surge of strength mingled with an excitement and energy that flowed through him, flush with a sense of drive and passion. Nevertheless, he had decided to take his time and savour this moment, relishing the experience of these life-changing few days. He wondered how many more cups of coffee he would have time for during the remainder of his existence, and it dawned on him that this would certainly be one of his last few. Steam rising from the mug diverted his thoughts to the impending explosion, Ahmed imagining the plumes of smoke that his destruction was surely going to cause soon, even very soon. Elvis turned to him with soppy wide eyes which clearly were prying: but what's all the weird stuff on the table, Master? Ahmed tapped his foot on the grubby carpet, his eye flickered briefly, and he took a long slurp of the comforting hot black liquid.

'Right, Elvis, shall we take a look at our new equipment, then? This lot is gonna change the way people look at the world, you mark my words,' he informed the dog, slowly rising to survey the contents of the suitcase which he had meticulously laid out . There, just as the girl had explained, were all the components for the bomb: a stubby battery, a short wire loom neatly tied with gaffer tape and connectors at each end, a tiny box with an LED light and switch, a glass vial of colourless liquid in a plastic frame, a larger package all wrapped up, various other leads/connections, and several A4 pages stapled together with printed instructions. Ahmed picked up the paperwork, before slumping into the sofa to slowly read in detail.

A while later, he sighed, itched his knee and set the papers down. He now understood his mission and saw that there was little time remaining. There was still one thing though that bothered him greatly: Elvis. The thought of leaving his trusty friend abandoned to a fate unknown weighed upon him, and troubled him. He could never imagine Elvis with another, it was not possible to even consider, especially as any new 'owner' (undoubtedly an Infidel) would certainly not be worthy of Elvis and his love. There was only one solution, clearly. He was to sacrifice his beloved canine companion before carrying out the mission in hand. He felt no grief, regret or even sorrow at this unexpected revelation, merely a sense of duty and responsibility to the tasks that he was compelled to undertake. He sat with his computer and, after some brief internet research, made up his mind to immediately go out to buy some cooking chocolate and rat poison. He found it harder and harder to look at Elvis, but his decision was beyond recall and he grabbed his coat en route for the shopping trip of doom. 'No Elvis, not this time,' he told the confused animal. 'You're staying in.' Elvis whined as the door to RonJoyce slammed firmly shut behind Ahmed.

Paul's mobile rang, electronically chirping a ridiculous jumble of sounds masquerading as a tune, concocted in a studio in Korea by the young and ambitious Kang Ji Seok who was handsomely rewarded (in South Korean Won) to create a few hundred ringtones every year. He jumped slightly, as the ring had become a rarer and rarer event. On the screen Tony's name appeared faintly. 'Oh, the ol' bastard,' Paul grumbled to himself as he took the call.

'Hello, Tony, how are you then, my friend?'

'Hi Paul. Well, everything seems okay my end, how's London life been treating you?'

Golf. A round of golf down in the countryside towards Havant, easy for Paul as he'd jump on the Waterloo-Portsmouth Harbour train line. He would hire some clubs down there, and Tony would take his own. The following week was looking promising . . . 'The Tuesday?' . . . 'Yep, that sounds fine' . . . 'Great, I'll pick you up at Havant station at midday, and we'll drive to Rowlands Castle from there, maybe a pub lunch on the way before an afternoon with the clubs, then a pint?' . . . 'Tony, that sounds wonderful, looking forward to it already, see you then. Bye.'

THE ROCK 'N' ROLL CHOIRBOY (AND HIS GIRLFRIEND).

He sits and eats his Cheese on Toast
Such a British snack
Preparing to conduct a Concert in Church
By watching a Fetish Porn movie.

She sits and Sucks her Thumb,
Nothing to do with the film, though
After 25 years of being either Drunk or Hungover
Sobriety is a far sight Trippier.

I say,
Discipline them with Milk!
YES, DISCIPLINE THEM WITH MILK!

By Yatter

Ahmed really couldn't sleep. At all. Elvis was downstairs writing in agony, whining and letting out chilling gurgling noises that Ahmed had never heard before. The combination of rat poison and chocolate, both in eat-as-much-as-you-dare quantities (and the dog had), was taking effect, and what effect! Ahmed lay motionless on his memory-foam mattress, snug in his 11-tog duvet with its British Home Stores duvet/pillow/sheet triple set in a simple magnolia, bought in the January sales of 1999. He hadn't washed any bedding for a couple of months, as he enjoyed the fug of his own smell mixed with the house's general stuffiness and dog staleness. The mix of too much coffee and the fact that his dog was suffering a protracted and clearly painful death below did not exactly aid his quest for sleep. However, at around 4:38 a.m., when all was quiet, Ahmed's brain was still racing even though he had just managed to get to sleep.

Rick Astley brushes past me in Aldershot town centre, just outside the WHSmith shop. I am delighted as he recognises me at once, and his gorgeous face reveals his unequivocal joy in seeing me.

RA: *Oh, Ahmed, my friend! We are friends, indeed! I have been searching high and low for you, here and there, long and far. And now I gather that you have been residing here, in Aldershot, for all of this time. If only I had known, I could have brought you hot sausages and other meaty snacks for breakfast, lunch, dinner . . . even midnight snack . . . every day. I need to nourish you, to give you strength and force for your mission, with the power that only quality meats can provide. But this is bothering me, there is something I need to know – my life is perfect apart from this burning desire to know, which is weighing me down. It's just . . . why didn't you tell me before about you residing here, in Aldershot?*

(At this interrogation, I feel awful. I really should have informed Rick about my whereabouts sooner, he was right. An awesome feeling of guilt envelops me like a duvet, a magnolia

duvet. I sink to one knee before Rick, an act of supplication that I really need him to appreciate).

Ahmed: *Rick, please forgive me. I'm so sorry, you can't know. I've been so busy, you see. I have unpacked my suitcase and emptied all the affairs. I've even been duty-bound to let Elvis eat too much, I think he's on his way now. He will be at Peace, so as my mission may be fulfilled.*

I have nothing else to say to Rick at this point. It doesn't matter as he always just seems to understand me naturally, words aren't always needed between us as he believes in me without judgement or criticism. He is just fantastic. There are never awkward silences between us, just time that passes as we relish our precious moments together. Shoppers pass by, engrossed in their consumerism and credit cards, yet at the same time no one is moving, and all that matters at this moment is my interchange with Rick. He smiles gently, and I melt. He's such a nice man, so gentle . . . and genuine too. His eyes meet mine, and I melt some more.

RA: *I'm not going to give up on you, nor do I intend to let you down in any way. I certainly won't desert you, Ahmed, as it now feels like we've know each other for a long time.*

Ahmed: *These are comforting and somehow familiar words. I thank you. Perhaps you should put them into song,* Rick*?*

Before he has the time to answer, Rick steps onto a low-flying cloud that fully obscures H&M, and even a part of the Clarks shoe shop – so much so in fact that I can only but glimpse a part of the kid's summer range at the far end of the window. I am aware that Rick is singing as the cloud moves away (perhaps even composing after listening to my songwriting encouragement, and taking my advice on board). I'd certainly like to think so. He is just amazing. He dances elegantly, as always, and I am sure that I smell sweet sausages . . .

Ahmed awoke, startled and stressed, penis flaccid. Sausages again? No . . . Elvis! He lept out of bed and raced down the fourteen stairs to RonJoyce's ground floor, where he found the animal asleep on the sofa. Not dead, just asleep, apparently breathing normally, even snoring gently. A mess of rancid dog vomit carpeted the carpet, its liquid portion mostly soaked into the fabric, leaving the remaining solid mass glistening disgustingly with its random formations and patterns, a sick painting ready to dry. Ahmed simply thought to himself, 'Ok, coffee first. Then I kill Elvis. No need to clean up the mess as I won't be around for much longer.' The kettle chugged into life, louder than usual, it seemed, and shaking a little, as the crescendo of its water-boiling efforts brought to mind a Boeing 747 preparing for take-off (this wonderful plane, the workhorse of the skies, that well-known, well-loved wide-body four-jet commercial airliner and cargo jet aircraft designed by Joe Sutter in the late 1960s) . . . until – *click*! – it's instant coffee time, followed by a simple canicide.

Joyce, Ahmed's late mother, had poor taste in, well, everything. One of the prize artefacts from her legacy that still remained in the house was a large bronze dog, which adorned the hallway of the property in the 1970s and hadn't moved until now. As it tumbled down onto Elvis' head at some speed there was a sharp crack as his skull crushed under its weight, the hefty item delivering a mighty blow to the sleeping canine. The dog was unaware, not even having time to waken before copious amounts of blood gushed from the disaster area that was once his head, flooding the sick-spattered carpet with a wash of red. Jelly-like brain matter spilled out onto the sofa, the animal's scraggy coat matted, flattened with liquid. Dog murder and carnage had come to Aldershot, and the room had looked better. Deflated, Ahmed retreated to his kitchen, rinsed his hands half-heartedly, sat down, and wept into his coffee. And wept. He hadn't realised that parting from Elvis would be so hard. Killing a whole bunch of human beings will be so much easier, he thought, and he wept some more.

UNTITLED, OR AM I?

Love is a thorn that
Cannot be parted
From Torn skin
Punctured by feeling,
A fractured heart
Still beating strong,
Though changing rhythm
To follow a different beat,
Less complex, yet still, towards
A new horizon.

To document life, as
The pen is mightier than the sword,
Fuck this . . .
Who writes poetry?

By Yatter

Sue was on the phone to her printer's in Portsmouth, who had just finished a first small run of *Time Management for the Worried Working Mum*, a modest introductory 250 copies. 'What I'll do is pick them up from you directly, there's absolutely no point in sending them to France when I'll be needing them in the UK to sell at the launch. Is that okay? I'll be over next week on the Monday flight, so if I come to you on the Tuesday around lunchtime, early afternoon, would that be okay? Brilliant. I'm so excited! And you've received the final artwork for *Confidence Starts in the Womb*, I hope? Great, well, that's fantastic. I look forward to seeing you next week then. Thanks . . . byee!'

'Fuck, that woman's annoying!' exclaimed Craig to John on hanging up the phone at Pompey Printers (at the top end of Sultan Road in Portsmouth, Hampshire). 'We should get a bit of dough out of her and her fucking self-help books though, it might end up being a bit of cash cow, you never know.'

'I'll let her know you called her that!' quipped John.

Back in France, Sue turned to Claude, glee written all over her face, lines and wrinkles of age fully activated.

'This is it, Claude, it's amazing. I'll go on Monday, stay with my sister in London, and get the train to the printer's on Tuesday. They're so nice, I spoke with a charming man called Craig. They'll already be doing a run of *Confidence* soon, as well. Then I'll see the solicitor on Wednesday morning, so I'll already be in town to go clothes shopping in the afternoon, ready for the launch on Thursday, and back here in the evening. I wish that you could come, mon amour.'

'Me as well, Sue, but as you know, with the animals it is not always so easy just to be leaving like this,' Claude explained.

In verity, the thought of leaving his farm and travelling to London absolutely terrified him, but he didn't want to let on. Sue was on a roll. 'You see, once it's all up and running, it should snowball. We'll get a buzz going about, some press, women's magazines and things, then we need to publish *Confidence* without messing about, within a couple of months. Then we'll push on and get *Menopause* out sharpish.' She was referring to *Miserable Menopause? I Don't Think So . . . !* Claude was, in fact, a little lost, but he was swept up with Sue's enthusiasm and energy.

'I will drive you to the airport, you know the SNCF are on strike again? Then, of course, we must hope that there is no industrial action by our friends in the Air Traffic Management.' He found her so independent, modern and vibrant, especially in comparison to his long-standing dowdy wife. She turned him on. 'A little *Pastis* to celebrate, no?' he suggested, grinning.

'You turn me on, my French lover!' she replied, attempting a sexy husky voice, having read his mind and previous thoughts. 'Make it a large one!'

Ahmed was calm, and Elvis was dead. The bomb was packed and primed and after praying for a while Ahmed felt strong, full of resolve. Leaving RonJoyce carefully (as he was carrying a bomb!), he stepped on the morning's untouched post which lay on the doormat, comfortable brown suede shoes (size 10 from BHS) leaving a dusty imprint on the reverse side of a letter. If he had stopped to look, he would have seen that the correspondence was stamped Atkins Greene Jones Solicitors, with a Croydon address.

'No need to water the vegetables today,' he told himself as he closed the garden gate, even allowing himself a vague grim grin.

Will bumped past a faceless commuter at Waterloo station, a duck with hoisin sauce wrap and sugary milky coffee in hand. A soft guitar case was casually slung over his shoulder and he was sporting some good fake Ray-Ban Wayfarers®. He considered himself to look pretty cool, and was looking forward to relaxing on the journey. With 15 minutes left until the train he ignored the multitude of shops and passed the barriers to stroll up the platform so as to bag himself a good seat at a window, preferably with a table and facing forwards. The rest of the band had left earlier in a tatty hired van with most of the gear including his pedalboard and amp, but due to a long-standing problem with his teeth Will had urgently needed to see a dentist that particular morning to sort out a niggling pain in one of his left-side molars. He was to meet up with them later, hopefully in time for the soundcheck. The destination was HMP Isle of Wight (formerly Parkhurst Prison), for a gig with The Prison Breakers. Easy enough – the train to Portsmouth, then a ticket to Ryde, IOW. (He'd suggested that they play that old Beatles song tonight, 'Ticket to Ride', but no-one else had been up for it.) He found a decent spot and sat down to eat. In the seat opposite there was a middle-aged woman speaking on her mobile, switching between English and bad French. She giggled before telling the person on the end of the line: 'Listen, mon amour, je te laisse because this must be costing a fortune and the train's going soon. Just make sure that our little beloved bonsai doesn't dry out, don't forget now, will you? Ok . . . oui, we speak soon, okay? Je t'embrasse fort. Je t'aime.' It was Sue, reassuring Claude back on his farm, who was already on his second Pastis of the day. She was on her way to Pompey Printers to pick up 250 copies of *Time Management for the Worried Working Mum*. Will thought that she seemed a bit annoying, and didn't wish to engage her in conversation.

He could hear *tap-tap-tap* on a laptop, an incessant clicking as if an electronic insect was hooked up to a nuclear charge. It was, in fact, the last-minute effort of a nervous Best Man putting the finishing touches on his speech for the weekend, still searching for appropriate stories and crowd-pleasing jokes. An occasional ring of a mobile would jostle for soundtrack space with the rustle of a nearby newspaper or a distant cry from an infant. A grown woman was angrily biting her nails right back to her wrists it seemed, lost in her digital world of tablet and banal American sitcom, navy headphones clasping her tiny skull. Then a guy who he couldn't see behind him suddenly started shouting at breakneck speed into his handset: 'Yep, it's me. Listen, it's a summary level piece, focusing the team into the project – standard 123/XYZ. Obviously, you'll present it to Jules before we take it to Marketing, the time scale's a bit tight but we can make this work,' (cough), 'excuse me. I know you don't have all the answers . . . yep, absolutely, absolutely. I was just wondering about the page-by-page skeletal team, could we ask about the slider, perhaps . . . you know, the fuzzy one!? Shit, why does tea on a train never taste quite right, is it the water? Anyway. Yep, that could work me thinks. Incentives, rewards . . . break it down into teams, make it *fun*, then we'll see how it goes. Brainstorm all the way, 'cos we need some meat on the bone before March, Collins will be breathing down our necks too no doubt, so I'll leave the ball in your court until I'm back. Ciao!' Will imagined what the guy must look like: nice smile, white teeth, fine clothes, charming manner (when necessary), clean hair and nails, interesting age (just nudging 30), clear complexion and slightly tanned skin, bright eyes, fair temperament, good job . . . aaggghh!

Will was becoming mildly irritated so turned his attention out the window to watch a train worker with a high visibility vest who was milling around on the platform doing, well . . . not much, it seemed.

Tony was often late, and today was no exception. He loved his car with a passion, a 1978 Mercedes W116 280S in light olive green which, despite some minor carburettor issues, was still running like a dream. He was looking forward to seeing Paul, the golf, some fresh air, a pint or two. His new red and white golf shoe sunk to the floor, accelerator sending the purr of the 6-cylinder engine up to more of a light but satisfying roar. Ignoring completely the 30mph traffic warning sign as he approached the bridge, Tony nudged 62mph as he fumbled with the Denon CD player to raise the volume from 12 to 29 (bass on + 1, treble on +2). He wanted to catch the tail end of Ian Kirkham's sax solo in a rare live version from 1999 of Simply Red's 'Money's too Tight to Mention'. As he crossed the pretty stone bridge, an extraordinary sight on his left caught his eye. A train was in the process of crashing, flailing off the tracks in all directions, an awesome force of weight, mass and speed chaotically hurtling forwards. Tony blinked, unaware that he too was unfortunately in the process of losing control and wiping out, distracted as he was by the shocking scene below. The final sounds that Tony heard – after 62 years of life on this earth – were Mick Hucknall singing about money (or the lack of it), screeching rubber on tarmac, a deafening bang, and finally his upper vertebrae violently cracking as he broke his neck after smashing into the unrelenting trunk of a 142-year-old oak tree at high velocity.

Ahmed was panting as he scrambled up the bank, startling an innocent blackbird with a broken wing that sat in a bush. Dazed, he powered over rocks and shrubs, negotiating thick patches of inhospitable brambles before clambering awkwardly over an unforgiving barbed-wire fence. Glancing down at his hands and legs he became aware of blood patches staining him, turning his trousers a warm wet camouflage. As well as a weird numb sensation there was a pervasive ache throughout his body, yet he couldn't perceive whether it brought him pain or pleasure. Any feeling he was experiencing flatly refused to transmit to or accurately compute in his brain. A pronounced dullness deafened his eardrums, all senses suspended as if he'd been heavily anaesthetised, mummified in glue. Ahmed was a man in a state of severe shock, face pale as chalk, feeling detached yet acutely aware at the same time, trance-like. Time felt suspended, unmoving. His hair was plastered onto sweaty forehead, dirt marking his left cheek above his unruly beard. A barren escarpment ahead of him led up sharply to a road leading off a bridge, but before tackling it he stole a glance back at the scene on the rail track. Mangled train carriages were strewn across the lines in a zigzag, some slewed over each other like discarded Lego bricks in a child's playroom. Shards of glass peppered the ground, and a number of windows were hanging precariously from their frames, smashed and fragmented yet somehow still holding together like shimmering jewelled jigsaw-puzzle pieces. As he looked down to survey the horrific carnage, Ahmed saw – but did not register – various limp human bodies scattered about, nor did he hear the rising groans coming from the injured, which blended curiously to form a macabre choir of agony. Dense white smoke was emanating from somewhere in the epicentre of the crash, acrid and harsh in the otherwise pure country air, and an uneasy stunned hush enveloped the atmosphere as if a damp blanket had cloaked the surrounding locality. The spectacular wreckage of the train – dramatically derailed and concertinaed – appeared to be almost in miniature, so surreal and implausible, an extravagant scene from a movie set. He paused as an uncontrollable tick forced his left eye to jerk with ludicrous and violent spasms, and he nodded his head in slow motion, taking it all in carefully, suddenly very aware of the fact that this was all his doing. This was the outcome of his actions, his intentions, an act initiated and carried out by him. The Lone Wolf had struck, almost without understanding. You see, he was neither a moral nihilist nor a bad man, but just quite simply a fucked-up cookie, that's all. Shielded within an eerie stillness all around, nobody noticed him as he turned to climb up to the road before brushing himself down and walking away. In his zombie-like state, Ahmed didn't even register the Mercedes 280S squashed and smoking at the base of the oak by the old bridge, Tony's lifeless form slumped like a crash-test dummy to the side of the steering wheel, strains of Simply Red still grooving through the smashed-up windscreen as blood dripped down its front wing. There was going to be no golf after all for Tony and Paul this particular afternoon as planned, or any other day, as the friends had 'left the building' within seconds and a few hundred metres of each other. Tony the car, Paul the train. They wouldn't even be able to attend each other's funerals. The wind picked up suddenly, a chilly gust transforming the towering oak branches overhead into a magical musical instrument as Ahmed slipped away across the fields on foot, seen by no-one.

Three hours after the crash, the media were reporting 89 deaths with 117 injured.

After seven hours, the toll had risen to 112 deaths and 144 injured.

Four days after the event the official numbers steadied at 114 deaths and 157 injured. Self-help Sue, guitar Will and golfing Paul were all named as victims.

After eight days, Mohammed Salil al-Liby (31) and Saif Fazul (36), both from Dagenham, were named as the train bombers after being arrested in an extensive night-time armed operation. Their faces were plastered all over the media for several months and the Prime Minister publicly labelled them as 'the cowardly masterminds and perpetrators of Britain's deadliest terrorist atrocity to date.' He continued, 'This country undoubtedly has one of the best security services in the world, if not the best, which is what enabled us to find the culprits of this ghastly act without delay and bring these terrorists into custody swiftly and efficiently. Justice will prevail, and these men will surely face a difficult future in the hands of our very capable Courts and Justice system. Our very clear message to these terrorists and those who aid or harbour them is that these arrests show that we will hunt you down, we are stronger and better-equipped than you, and we will not give in or cease our fight against such evil when confronted by such barbaric and unjustifiable acts.'

At the Pearly Gates there are long tables, thousands of them, in fact, as far as the eye can see. Each table has twelve people sitting around it, all being served. At our table sit Paul, Tony, Sue and Will, as well as a number of others. At the head is Rick Astley and at the other end is the legendary English footballer from years ago, Paul Gascoigne. Sue toys with a hunk of bread, before turning to Paul and quietly informing him, 'Paul, I'm having a strange dream.'

'No Susan, not a dream. This is the most concrete, real experience of your entire existence. Relax, there will be fish served very soon, and Rick and I are here to guide you.'

'Is there no meat on the menu?' Will enquired.

'William, this is a purely fish supper for us to all enjoy together in these beautiful surroundings. You will eat the most heavenly conga steaks from our pure heavenly seas, the likes of which have never passed your lips. There is bread and as much water as you care to drink, but no vegetables and certainly not any meat. I am sure that you will enjoy everything on offer, William.' Paul explained the situation clearly in dulcet tones.

At the other end of the table Rick was also clarifying a few points to his fellow diners:

'Pure fish from the cleanest heavenly oceans will help to purify your souls. Paul and I are your hosts, ready to guide you all through the gates to your final destination.' The guests ate in silence, respectfully finishing everything on their plates aside the bones, before sitting patiently, serene smiles on their faces. After a certain amount of time had passed, Rick calmly spoke, just one word. 'Good.' He nodded gently to Paul Gascoigne, ex-footballer.

A cloud descended over the entire table, engulfing the assembled company. The meal had come to a close.

And thus the crowds at the Pearly Gates ate their fill and were glad!

Meanwhile, back in Aldershot, Ahmed had shaved his beard. Unable to comprehend how he could possibly have survived the train bomb, nothing made any sense anymore. It also seemed incredible that nobody had come to arrest him. 'The words *chase*, *goose* and *wild* spring to mind,' he remarked to himself while watching the police talking about the bombing on the news. He only just remembered priming the bomb in the toilet before walking up the train carriage, the next memory being an endless journey over fields and through woods. Vague memories of shelter under a bush for several hours of semi-sleep. Somehow he had made it back to Aldershot undetected, perhaps under the cover of unintentionally looking much like a tramp. The homeless don't blow up trains now, do they? Deadened inside, numb yet sensitive, confusion reigned in his head. He felt incapable, impotent, vulnerable . . . resigned to a certain fate as if trapped in the dentist's chair, sinking backwards in desperation. Hair was attached through skin. His skull housed his brain, and his brain housed a jumbled labyrinth of dark thoughts, feelings, phobias, ideas racing past broken diodes, perished solder, twisted transformers and through tiny doors that should have remained firmly shut. Mental chaos was Lord. Treacle brain and fug here, lightning thoughts there. He had an overwhelming feeling that his time as Ahmed had come to an end, and he wanted to revert back to Peter. His previous years as a Christian of some sort hadn't worked out, and his recent dabbles in Islamist Fundamentalism seemed to be rather destabilising and difficult, to say the least. He would have to seek out a new way, a different path. Yes, that's it, Peter Pilgrim is his name now . . . none of this Ahmed nonsense, I mean, look at the maelstrom of trouble it causes!

I am on all fours, aware of noises emanating from over my shoulder. Gruff grunting and an irregular panting. I steal a glance, only to see a flushed Rick Astley sweating profusely behind me, wearing a pained expression. He has lost his usual poise and composure that I have come to adore. I notice a pile of items on the otherwise bare floor – it's a discarded clown costume and mask, a red nose flashing uselessly. I suddenly understand that we are in an abattoir, but all appears to be quite in order, exactly as it should be. Between sharp intakes of breath, RA *repeats over and over: 'There's good meat there, there's good meat there!' I don't really understand what's going on, why I'm here or what we are doing, but that's okay and I don't really mind. It's fine by me.*

A sharp stinging sensation awakens my senses, a pain in my anus. I realise that RA *is mercilessly penetrating me with a comedy-style Tom and Jerry stick of dynamite. The dirty, cheeky swine! I awake with a jolt!*

Meanwhile, a letter from Atkins Greene Jones Solicitors lies open on the kitchen table, while a dead dog lies open in the living room. The smell was intensifying by the hour. It had been nearly two weeks since the *event*, and in these two weeks Peter had barely slept, barely eaten, and had remained virtually like a prisoner under voluntary house arrest in RonJoyce. Today, however, a rainy Tuesday like any other, something happened: Peter came to, back into the world of some kind of reality – his own. He decided to clean up the fetid living room and dispose of the dog's putrid body. A couple of hours later he returned from Elvis's final resting place – the vegetable patch – covered in blood, earth and muck. He took a long shower and finally put on some clean clothes, even changing his bedding for a fresh set. In the freezer he found an Iceland meal for one, Beef Roast Dinner (with potatoes, vegetables, a Yorkshire pudding and gravy, £1.80). A long 8 minutes later, after the microwave's pure ping, he was sat at the kitchen table greedily attacking the shiny offering off its plastic tray packaging. The overpowering smell of bleach didn't even put him off as he hadn't eaten for days, and he ate in seconds, not minutes, despite the intense heat. A while later, he was back in the same chair with an instant coffee, staring wide-eyed at the letter in his hand, disbelief written over his pale face.

26th September,
Atkins Greene Jones Solicitors
35–37 The High Street
Croydon
CRO 1GL

Your Ref: Mr. PILGRIM, Peter
Our Ref: TH46-8D41

Dear Mr.Pilgrim,

Re: The Estate of the Late Terrence Walters:
79 Church Street, Croydon CR0 4ST
Walter's Quality Meats, 149 High Street, Croydon CR0 1GT, (including 149a & 149b)

Please allow me to introduce myself . My name is Jonathan Greene, a Senior Partner of Atkins Greene Jones Solicitors. I am the Executor of your late Uncle Terrence Walter's Estate as above and please accept my and this firm's condolences on your loss. It is my duty as your Uncle's Executor to advise you that you are the Principal Beneficiary of his Last Will and Testament.

You are to inherit his house in Church Street, and in addition his butcher's business operating from the address above, including the residential apartments situated above the shop. I have received two out of the three valuations that I am required to obtain for the purposes of obtaining Probate, and the combined value of the properties is estimated at c £1,600,000 to £1,700,000.

I should be grateful if you would please contact me personally on my direct line (0208 726 5156) to discuss further and to arrange a mutually convenient time that we might meet at this office in order to discuss matters further.

I look forward to hearing from you.

Yours faithfully,
Jonathan Greene (Senior Partner).
Atkins Greene Jones Solicitors, Croydon.

Uncle Terrence had been his mother Joyce's younger brother, who Peter had a vague memory of meeting many years previously, perhaps as a teenager. His mother had rarely spoken of him, and Peter hadn't even thought about him for years. He had no idea why Joyce and Terrence hadn't remained close, and had no recollection of any stories or facts about the deceased. The last time their paths had crossed had been at Joyce's funeral many years ago, and Peter tried without success to recall if they had even had a conversation. So why had the inheritance come to him? Was nephew Peter the only relative, Terrence perhaps having no friends and feeling duty-bound to keep everything in the family? Peter sat back slowly in the Ikea chair SKOGSTA and sighed, resting the letter back on the table and looking at his trembling hands, his thoughts scrambled even further.

The hideous fluorescent lamps overhead flickered periodically. That, combined with the sound of various slams and bangs, made for a real sense of unease within the band. It was the evening of the day of the train's bombing. The Prison Breakers were again getting their fill of prison food, sat around a Formica table in a canteen usually reserved for guards. Shepherd's pie with strange rounded carrots (were they tinned ?) followed by apple crumble and some very sweet runny custard. They had finished a rather stressful soundcheck in the prison hall, and Will the guitarist hadn't shown up yet. Dave was pissed off.

'He hasn't fuckin' shown up, and he hasn't even fuckin' texted me to let me know where he is, the twat,' he grumbled yet again.

'No-one heard anything?'

The guys shook their heads.

'Listen dude, we'll get through this evening and then it's all good, so don't stress, mate,' Baz helpfully replied through a mouthful of dry mashed potato. He was referring to the fact that Will was going to get the sack from The Prison Breakers in the van on the way back to London the following day, so one last gig didn't really matter. A mobile message alert went off. Baz put his knife down and nonchalantly checked the screen, hoping that it was a girl. It wasn't, it was his mother.

Hi dear, just checking in with you. I saw on the news that there's been a terrible terrorist bomb they think, on a train. You okay, honeybum?

'Oh shit, there's been some terrorist shit on a train or something, loads dead,' he announced to the band over their dinner. 'The wankers don't let up, do they?'

Not one of the group even considered the fact that Will

might have been on the train, it just didn't even cross their minds.

The gig went ahead that evening at 8:30 p.m. sharp, with the keyboard player massively overcompensating for the lack of guitar. It was a shit concert in a shit venue, but the inmates loved it. Just after coming off stage and taking a large swig from a warm bottle of Coke, Dave suddenly said,

'Guys, you don't suppose Will could've been on that train, do you?'

Baz's immediate cutting reply was, 'Well, at least you won't have to sack him if he was!'

They all laughed, a little nervously.

Will's body had in fact been practically vaporised by the force of the explosion from the device in the train's toilet, and he would never strum his guitar again for The Prison Breakers or any other pop/rock combo outfit, for that matter. Dave had been right.

Claude rarely watched TV. This evening, though, Sue was away, he had knocked back one or two too many Pastis. He felt tired after the day's chores around the farm. The sassy Katia Durand was his favourite newscaster on TF1, and there she was almost ranting about Marine Le Pen's continual rise throughout France, especially in the countryside (aided largely by a high proportion of ill-educated followers, although that was not reported). He loved Katia's low-cut top and the fact that she was a touch over made-up. The piece concluded and images of a train crash taken from a helicopter flashed across the screen. He turned the sound up a bit more to discover that it had been a terrorist attack in the UK that very afternoon, on the London-Portsmouth train, with many fatalities.

'Mais non, ce n'est pas possible. Putain de merde!' he spluttered to no-one but himself.

The phone was on the table, and he hadn't heard from Sue since after lunch. He composed himself, beset by limerence and concern, and dialled her mobile after finding the number in the handset's memory. Nothing, not even the answerphone, just silence.

'Non, non, ce n'est pas possible!'

In the kitchen, his unsteady hands helped to make the Pastis a double shot. The smallest drop of water from the tap was added, 'une larme.' Claude sniffed as he opened the freezer for a couple of chunks of ice. 'Mais, ce n'est pas possible!' for the third time.

It *was* indeed possible, and a few days later Claude had the news that he so dreaded confirmed via Tom (still officially Sue's husband), who in turn had received official confirmation of Sue's death from the French Embassy in Paris. That evening, along with Keith, the three men managed to polish off nearly *eight* bottles of red wine, no problem. An uxorious Claude's emotional outpourings suddenly became aggressive rants at around midnight, before he became an early victim and was asleep on the sofa by 1 a.m. Keith later sprawled out on a chaise longue in the garden, with Tom at last passing out on the cold hard floor of Claude's farmhouse kitchen. Despite the terrible noise that they'd made over several hours, the night seemed almost horizontal now, still and flat as a forgotten wind-shielded pond lost deep in a Canadian forest. Only the occasional snores of the unlikely trio of drunken men broke the silence.

The following morning The Three Musketeers – hungover, stinking and slightly embarrassed – drank coffee together in near silence. Claude was already smoking. The UK contingent sheepishly said their goodbyes to Claude before setting off, and once they'd left Claude immediately had a plan. He needed his wife. Now, right now. One can only imagine the double shock that was to follow. He soon discovered in town that his wife was no longer living with her sister, but had recently moved in with Brigitte above her boulangerie (where over the years she had won several prizes for stunning Vienoisseries, and a very special mention for her delicious Paris Brest). Brigitte was a 50-something, slightly batty divorcee in fine physical form, who was now having a full-blown relationship with Claude's wife of 30 years. His lover Sue was dead and his wife was now having a lesbian affair in his local town with an expert cake maker, and she didn't even have a sweet tooth! The sorrow and the shame, what humiliation! That very afternoon, Claude entered his main barn for the last time, inchoate rage bursting through every neuron. The events that had come to pass were clear even through his hungover mind, or so he thought, and he kicked some mud then carefully smoothed his eyebrows with the knuckle of his index finger. *Who would water and watch over Sue's bonsai tree now?* The sad farmer methodically loaded the shotgun, which once belonged to his father, sat on a bale of hay, sighed heavily and placed the end of the barrel in his mouth without hesitation. He looked upwards, and realised that he had emptied his brain of thoughts, perhaps due to some kind of involuntary auto-protect mechanism, a type of partial brain shutdown. This was good, and he felt momentarily at peace. A sudden bang sent nesting swallows off in all directions, somewhere in the distance a dog barked, and it was a few seconds before a disturbed silence resumed once more.

One thousand two hundred and thirty-six days later . . .

Peter sat in his office. A coffee, forgotten for a while, was getting cold and undrinkable on the desk. The inherited property in Croydon had sold swiftly for a mouth-watering price, and even after taxes and expenses Peter was now a wealthy man. A portion of his new-found wealth was invested in a business venture named The Peace of Meat Ltd. Peter's immediate regret after what he considered to be his *accident* (the bombing of a train and murder of many innocents) was like that of a confused Brexiteer a couple of days after voting: bitter. He had a fresh mission, and it seemed to be working. Inspired by his family connections to the meat trade, Peter now invested all his energy in packaging supposedly halal meat to export to mainly European markets – Germany principally – but also France, Norway, Belgium, Italy, and even the Middle East. It was his glorious revenge. None of the meat was halal at all, so he took pleasure in the fact that he was essentially 'poisoning' hundreds of thousands of people. Just as with the bombing, he was so blasé that he somehow continued to get away with it, despite Council inspections and controls. The halal sticker was always the last process, in an area partly hidden towards the back of the processing plant. He loved coming to work, and had a list up on a board of the other possible names of the company, before he had decided on The Peace of Meat Ltd.

Halal Heaven Ltd.
Muslim Meats Ltd.
Muslim Mutton Ltd.
No More Pork Pies, Just Halal Lies! Ltd.
Hungry Halal Cuts Ltd.

Passionate Pure Meats Ltd.
Mostly Muslim Meatz Ltd.
Meet my Meat Ltd.
Massage my Meat Ltd.
Meat: A Love Story
Meat is my Murder Ltd.

The Peace of Meat Ltd. sits at the back of the nondescript industrial estate on the edge of Aldershot town, which had for a few years been spreading like a tumour across the surrounding countryside. It was a comfortable ten minutes away by car from RonJoyce, maybe fifteen on a bad day. Having taken out a twelve-year commercial lease on Units C47 and C48, Peter was governing an impressive space of several hundred draughty metres squared, which housed a kitchen and canteen room, the factory floor with all sorts of conveyor belts and hooks, hanging contraptions, clunky machinery, giant refrigeration units, and two spacious offices. It resembled a W. Heath Robinson drawing, but in real life. The icy toilets reminded him of school days, an impression strengthened by the incomprehensible writing scrawled on the back of the cubicle doors. On one side of the buildings Unit C46 housed a Perspex suppliers, and the smaller unit to the right appeared to be something to do with pharmaceuticals. The people who occasionally came in or out were strangely aloof and distinctly unfriendly. This, however, suited Peter down to the ground so he adopted a rather similar attitude towards the plastic guys of C46. Thus, privacy was maintained by all. Ample parking and satisfactory night time security - good lighting and a 24-hour team of two men and a dog - convinced Peter that he had found a great spot for his meaty activities. Business was brisk, and meat was selling in huge quantities. In fact, it was even proving difficult to keep up with the ever-growing demand as the company grew and orders increased. People around the world were hungry, and sought meat. Peter wasn't just going to be a rich man, he was destined at this rate to become a very wealthy one. He had no qualms whatsoever about the scale of death involved, the animal blood on his hands, and actively relished the fact that he was poisoning so many populations with his pretend halal products. He really was a sicko.

Here in the office the coffee was now cold as Peter had dozed off in his Director's chair. This was to be the moment for his last dream and message from mentor and friend, Rick Astley.

RA: *Ah, Peter, what a pleasure. You appear serene in your new calling, but you must not work too hard. You seem tired, my friend. Sleeping on the job . . . it's not a particularly professional approach, if you don't mind me saying. Have you been eating properly, Peter? I have some organic pork chops, sourced from a very special place. I have also procured a pot of Bavarian sweet mustard, just delicious with this good meat.*

Peter says silent, unable to reply. RA starts to turn the chops on his barbecue that is smoking more than usual today. He appears to be singing, gently gyrating his hips as he elegantly tends to the meat, deep in concentration. Life is fine, and the two men are content in each other's company. Suddenly RA lifts skywards on his barbecue cloud, and a never-ending gilt staircase is somehow placed just behind him, at the same time as a white acoustic guitar floats down from above. RA caresses the strings, his complexion flawless, his face just radiant. No-one has ever heard 'Stairway to Heaven' played so delicately, so magically. A bearded figure stands on the staircase, and addresses RA *gently over the music:*

Bearded Figure: What is the query that you have come to put to me, my boy?

RA *stops playing and looks up to the man, a tear in his eye. There is a slight pause before he replies, a false confidence almost cracking his velveteen speaking voice, like somebody saying their marriage vows, desperate to speak clearly and well.*

RA: *May I furnish you with mustard on your sausage, Jesus?*

Bearded Figure: Congratulations! That is correct, my Son. Come, come. Enter the land of Celestial Virgins, of Good Meat and Plentiful Pork! Rise up.

RA: *oh yes, there's Good Meat there . . . Heavens Above! I never knew that there would be real Celestial Virgins available with you, Jesus. I thought that that particular package was only available with the other Operator.*

Bearded Figure: My Virgins are cleaner and better-looking than those of the other Operator, although I will not speak ill of them. You will not be disappointed. Rise, my Child, come into the Light. I will wash your feet before nourishing you plentifully with pork. You need to eat well, in order to give you maximum strength for the Virgin Pool, so you can give of your best.

Jesus reaches out to RA, *large hands outstretched – those perfect nails – eyes wide and welcoming. Colours all look filtered.* RA *mounts the staircase slowly, the cloud, barbecue, guitar are gone. The staircase and two faraway figures drift away.*

Peter work up with a start. No erection this time. He knew that RA *had left him for good this time, and he welled up too, before wearily picking up his coffee mug and placing it in the microwave.*

Over 4,000 miles away, Brian was sweating. A lot. He washed his face with cold water then splashed his neck liberally with a heroic aftershave. His canary (named Coalmine, or Minnie for short) was tweeting away in a cage in the corner of the immense marble and gold en-suite bathroom. He was hanging out in the white mansion that he'd bought for a perfectly reasonable 7,500,000 US Dollars from a world-renowned Afro-American boxer (who also sweats a lot). The A/C was on max, but Brian just couldn't get used to the climate, and found the heat suppurating, oppressive. He had just ushered two hookers to a waiting taxi after a disgraceful cocaine-fuelled sex binge. Misty was a gorgeous brunette with a dynamite body, Candy a tall black girl who was barely 21 and rocking some crazy peroxide blond hair. She also rocked some serious Lois Lane glasses. The girls had been provided as a 'duo package' by Atlanta's Angels Agency, and Misty performed 'all services' (at a price) . . . not so the case with Candy, who would not indulge in full sex. She had sucked him off fairly well with a condom while Misty hovered around in her stockings, but for Candy the games stopped there. Her explanation was that she 'didn't want to be unfaithful to her boyfriend'. This was a mildly warped reasoning given her choice of profession, thought Brian, yet he accepted her rules and looney logic, especially as Misty more than made up for her partner's shortfalls. Misty was generous and very willing and he considered her to be built for comfort. They were in the opulent master bedroom, a fine example of hideous nouveau riche bad taste: all velvet, tassels, mirrors, gold and gigantic plasma TV. Bryan Adams' '(Everything I Do) I Do It For You' drifted out from invisible speakers somewhere. As the girls surveyed the room, Brian observed:

'Well, you know he fucked Lady Di?'

'Who?' asked Candy with her squeaky voice.

'This guy . . . Bryan Adams,' Brian explained about his namesake.

'Lucky Princess Di!' quipped Misty. Then she suddenly looked serious. 'Brian, these ugly mutts aren't gonna stay here and watch, surely? It's weirding me out already.'

She was referring to the horrible dogs that were sat on a dog bed in the corner, stinking and panting. Brian was attempting to assume his role as a bit of a nasty man – they were called Donald (Trump), Nigel (Farage) and Brian Jnr.

'Oh yeah. Don't worry, they're fine, they don't mind!' he replied, completely missing her point. She decided to let it go and to try to ignore the ugly mutts. She forced a smile. Candy was in her own world, rubbing her long hands over the pile of cushions on the bed, admiring the soft furnishings.

'Look at that piece!' Brian was pointing at a hideous gold bust of Donald Trump, one of his heroes. 'I can't remember how much it cost me, but it was the best however-much-it-cost-me that I've ever spent!' he laughed forcefully.

Candy really was in a world of her own. 'Cushions are one of my three favourite things. Cushions, penguins and chips!' Brian and Misty exchanged a glance.

'O – kay!' remarked Misty with sarcasm, kicking off her shoes.

Soon, Misty's luscious thick tongue found its way deep into Brian's left ear and she licked all around for a good minute. On pulling out, she whispered almost inaudibly into the wet cavity, 'If I rub coke all over your bell-end, will you rub some on my pussy?' Brian acquiesced like a well-behaved child as he considered this proposition a wonderful idea. He didn't know it at the time, but this was certainly the defining moment that was to lead to a long-term and deep addiction to hookers and cocaine, generally together. In fact, he learnt to love them both in equal measure, and found the combination nothing short of glorious! The winning formula. Was this the ultimate Schadenfreude, his misuse of human beings in such a manner? Now on their way out, the girls both had large wads of cash in their tiny handbags, alongside condoms, make-up, mobiles and house keys. Candy sneezed suddenly; a cocaine sneeze – a massive unladylike blowout. Brian slowly made the sign of the cross as benediction, enjoying briefly reliving his time as head of The Section. 'Bless you,' he purred, the softly ironic smile revealing recently-polished gnashers. Then at once Misty gasped as she twisted somehow and fell on the sand-coloured chippings of the immaculate driveway.

'Ow, my fucking Jimmy Choos!' she squealed, picking up a broken heel, shoe in two pieces.

'Here,' purred Brian, 'this should do it.' He peeled off five or six hundred dollar bills from a roll he magically produced from somewhere on his person.

'Thanks, doll,' replied Misty a minute later through the taxi window as it pulled away. 'Don't do anything I wouldn't!'

She grinned widely, eyes taught open, flashing that perfect American white smile, framed by those naughty full lips and brash pillar-box red recently-reapplied raucous lipstick. The Armenian cabbie drove off with end-of-shift weariness, tyres softly crunching on the stones as they made their way down to the iron gates which slid open automatically to let them through , back Downtown.

'Jesus, they're hot!' gurned Brian through his tense jaw, as the taxi driver stole furtive glances of the working girls with his sparrow eyes in the rear-view mirror, thinking exactly the same thing.

'Jesus, what a loser!' Misty hissed to Candy after a minute.

'Yeah, another sad case,' agreed Candy, stifling a yawn. 'Only thing he's got going for him is all that money.'

'I dunno,' disagreed Misty. 'He does get some really good coke and I still adore that cute British accent. You can't trust a man with no vices, and he's sure got a few. Yeah, but he's an asshole!' she concluded, as they both giggled girlishly.

Brian passed the faux Greek columns and breezed through the black, highly-glossed front door.

'Thanks to you, The Section. I am the One Mighty and Great Prophet . . . give me all your cash, you pathetic losers!' he cried out to nobody as he crossed the oak-floored hallway, grinning from ear to ear. Buzzing around the velvet-clad living zone, he mumbled, preparing another enormous line of top-grade coke with his black credit card.

'What's this we've got for breakfast then, eh? Full English, is it? Come to Daddy!' At this he snorted massively up each nostril, hesitated, then leant back into the blue leather sofa before clicking on the over-sized plasma TV. He let rip an angry fart, then suddenly jumped up as if all was not well and strode into the kitchen to get a chilled bottle of French Champagne out of the French Champagne fridge. 'It's fine,' he explained out loud to himself, returning to the sofa. 'I only suffer from a hangover if I *mix* Champagne with whisky.' Beads of cold sweat were forming on his brow, his eyes were like marbles and his heart pounded like a 1990's techno track. He loved to watch the Bible preachers, crazed money-grabbers encouraging the weak to send in their hard-earned money, phone numbers flashing across the bottom of the screen as the kind man insists that viewers donate to his Pentecostal New Church of Hope.

'Now that's how to do it . . . go on, my son!' encouraged Brian through gritted teeth, knee bouncing up and down in glee. He remembered the glory days of The Section and Polly's face flashed in front of him. After Misty and Candy she seemed so frumpy and dull, and he briefly wondered how she was coping. Very briefly. He had managed, with her unwitting help, to expand The Section's influence – along with its sudden revenue flow – to a degree that had shocked even himself. The online presence had helped enormously (Polly's idea and mainly managed by her), and it had been very hard to know when to cut and run, before becoming too greedy. People had even sold their houses to give him cash; he must've had some kind of magic touch. Polly's father Tony had died in some strange event . . . some kind of terrorist thing involving a train that had been blown up, and it had made him crash his car or something. When Polly received her inheritance, Brian only had to suggest that it came to The Section, and she arranged just that. She had received half as the rest was for her druggie brother Norman, who, at least for now, seemed to have disappeared off the radar . . . something about India, was it? Brian had jumped into overdrive mode at that point, aiding with the liquidation of Tony's assets: three vintage cars, a sprawling estate in Surrey, lots (and lots) of shares, a mansion in the hills of Umbria, a business to sell and a fair packet of cash in the bank. Once this was done Brian realised that enough was enough and that the time had come. By the day on which Brian disappeared he had managed to stash away an unbelievable sum of money, hidden from authorities or any other prying eyes through a complex system of multiple companies and trusts, to the tune of millions of pounds. The Cayman Islands had never seemed so inviting, even if just for his shady business in the sunny îles. Hopes dashed, lives ruined, beliefs shattered . . . Brian didn't care about all of that. The cult of The Section crumbled as its members and supporters came around to the realisation that they had been massively conned, duped and left hanging. Yet He, Their Glorious Leader, had triumphed and managed to live his dream (even if he had since become the classic example of the depressed millionaire), and that's what this was all about, so there we are, it's all good, that was the plan, and that's it, all's well that ends well, stick *that* in your pipe and smoke it, and why not, do I give a shit?

IAN, WHAT DO YOU WANT?

Ian Somnia why do you follow me so?
It's 4 a.m. and the lights are low
Your presence is grating, and
My patience is wasting.
Go and bother someone else
There are folk that perhaps it helps -
The early shift, a postman perhaps?
Or seek out lovely Sally Somnia
But leave me alone before I collapse!

By Yatter

Yatter was stone broke but happy. His compilation of prose and poetry was coming along in leaps and bounds, and his new Bad Poet's Society site and blog had already attracted eight followers. He had taken over the flat, even Norman's room, as it appeared that the Electric Dwarf really had disappeared off the face of the earth and wasn't coming back. Nothing, not even a postcard. This meant that Yatter was now paying double the rent, but he was just about managing, and for now he enjoyed the privacy and extra space without Ed, so it was worth it. Yatter had been to the police at the time to report the little man's disappearance, only to discover that Polly had already done so after their latest chat on the phone. He hadn't really felt that the police were particularly bothered, and anyway, he's Polly's brother and she's dealing with all of that now. The flat was now in order, a different spot to when Norman had been living there: clean sink and dustbin, sofa clear of rubbish, no unidentifiable odours lingering – perhaps just that of bleach – and no drugs! The mystery surrounding the disappearance of Norman/Edward continued: it's just known that he was probably somewhere in India, but even that's not certain. Around a year ago, a known Polish criminal was arrested in Italy using a doctored version of Norman's passport, but he refused under questioning to disclose how or where he had procured it, so this one and only lead was effectively a dead end. Yatter had mindlessly thrown out any post for Norman after a couple of months, it always appeared so unimportant: publicity from banks, store card offers, mobile phone upgrade leaflets, letters from a Solicitor to inform Norman that he was now an extremely wealthy man with half of his father Tony's inheritance . . . just that kind of thing; nothing of any importance.

THE APPENDIX: (IT'S OBVIOUS TO ME)

I've no time for conventional twits
Who denounce any function of the appendix.
For me it hides something, buried like a mole
Could it not be the perfect sack for our Soul?

By Yatter

The Electric Dwarf had started to look like an Indian, and a poor one at that. In a year's time he would become a strange relic of a being drifting through life, ghosting out the rest of his existence. He would become disgustingly thin, desperately ill-looking like a matchstick man in a Lowry painting, living off the generosity of others – the brave few who weren't scared away by his appearance. The skin and bone crew. His smell too would become a serious issue, body stinking to high heaven, with his brain in an even higher dimension. Even his own sister Polly – if she ever were to manage to find him and track him down – would struggle to recognise her own flesh and blood, the scrag that Norman would soon morph into. Now, however, he had come to India for his two-week holiday, with the fantastic plan of having his 'one last blow-out' on drugs before straightening himself out. It hadn't quite worked out like that. He was to become passport-less, shoeless, sanity-less.

It had started at the airport where he quickly tracked down the bar, where people from all time zones drank at all times of the day and night. Ed was perched on a bar stool with a glistening pint of Guinness and a double Jamesons backing it up. In a psychological chicken-and-egg analysis he was struggling to ascertain whether:

A: He was drinking now due to a stressful journey to the airport.

B: He had had a stressful journey to the airport in order to reward himself with a drink on arrival.

OR

C: He just likes drinking.

Rue the day that Ed met Barry a couple of days after his arrival. Barry was a slim question mark of a man with a Mancunian accent and some bad tattoos, who wore dreadlocks despite being white.

His dirty red T-shirt proclaimed:

Sex
Murder
Art

Barry had an annoying habit of speaking out of the side of his mouth, as if he had suffered a stroke (he hadn't). This, combined with his accent, sometimes made it hard for Ed to fully understand what he was saying, but as most of it was nonsense or quite simply dull he wasn't particularly bothered. Barry had given Ed a couple of tabs of LSD as they drank a couple of beers at lunchtime, lounging around under a palm tree. They were the same, these two innocent-looking small squares of blotting paper adorned with a rough image of Kermit the Frog. After the fourth large beer and a cocktail called The Bee Sting, well-aided by a little Dutch courage and Barry's insistent banter, Ed gingerly placed a tab on his tongue. A few minutes later, as Barry was taking a piss somewhere around the back of the bar, Ed took the second tab. 'Oh fuck it, why not!?' he said out loud to himself.

Barry returned, Ed flashed him the peace sign – or did he mean number two?

'No, you didn't, did you, Norm?' questioned Barry, feigning concern for his new 'friend'.

Ed just nodded, a silly little smile forming on his sun-damaged, cracked dry lips. The odd small human, becoming odder.

'Fuck man! You'd better put your seatbelt on my friend, even one of those bad boys is pretty strong.' And with this, Barry stood up and briskly left the bar mumbling something out of the corner of his mouth, not turning back, and leaving his drinks bill for the soon-to-have-left-the-planet Electric Dwarf to settle. Their paths were never to cross again.

Norman had taken acid. He started to feel weird after 10 miNutes or so. He was fully weird after 25 minutes. A truleee sTroNg Wave CaMe afTer ABooT 40 mIutes. WAve, lIKe on tHE beeecH. DAvE the WAve. dAve tHe RaVe. I WavE 2 da BArMan BuT HiS arM DiScoNn eCCx. AcTuAlLy DisConnEcTS, oUt aNd AwAy fRom THe ARm soCk Ett. BuT thEn iTz Back In aGAin, ooooo mY arM is so hEAvEE. ThIs GaY IndiAn Has a NEfArioUs TeMpER. BuT itz NoT mY faUlT, I ExxPlanE. I eXplaIn foR HourS, ManeE hOurs. eX PLaNe, a PlAne fLiEZ aWay, bak 2 lOndOn toWn. I'LL shoW u gOod TyMes, Then You'Ll C, LiTZ r So BriTe no Need 2 fiTe, MOve DesE sHoez, I aIn't gOt dA Bloooossss. I nEed a lisT tO sORt mySelF oUt:

wiFi

aLL LiEs

piGeons faLLiNg fRom tHe SKy, iTZ eNouGh 2 maKe u CrY

bUt I, I jUsT fRy, bAkinG liKe aPPle PiE.

sHe talKZ wIth pEoPle wHo'd lIsTen

wIthOut the fAinTesT aDmiSSiOn

%##3 10010000110110100100010 %

oH nO, fOOd EjEcTINg mY pErsoN, aRmy, ArmY. E mer Gen Ceeee.

Food was indeed ejecting out of Ed's mouth, or, more precisely, warm beer was. The time was now about 9 p.m. and he was alone on a second-floor balcony somewhere, leaning on the thick bamboo of a surprisingly smooth, warm and comfortable window ledge. Deep in his muddled brain, the hot vomit spewing out of his foul oral cavity was turning into 7cm-high military figures in shiny green plastic with moulded bases. Loads of guys, all ready for action – maybe an entire platoon of men, around 50 men. Their parachutes thankfully all opened and they raced to the ground below safely. The silky parachutes made amazing 3D patterns as they fluttered downwards, light reflecting in all directions. There were no casualties, just Norman.

ShE wAs iN thE KEecHAn peeLinG hArd-bOileD eGgS. lOokIng GooD.

'wHaT r u UpTo iN tHe kItcHen tHen?'

I aSkEd.

'WeLL, I'M pEeliNg HaRd-BoIled eGgs' sHe rePlieD.

'pLeaSe uSe thE RunNy yOlk oF aN eGG tO rEmoVe a CoFfeE sTaiN, pLeaSe lOve mE do, oH mY sWedIsh VolVo IdoL, mY VolVo IdoL'

Oscar Wilde once reported that 'It's an odd thing, but anyone who disappears is said to be seen in San Francisco. It must be a delightful city and possess all the attractions of the next world.' Norman had indeed disappeared, and it was an odd thing. In keeping with the fact that he always did get everything a bit wrong, he was not however in San Francisco, but getting on for around 10,000 miles away. Norman was back on the beach at an unknown hour on a random day, somewhere near the Equinox Café. He saw an old Indian man of middling height that he didn't know who appeared to approach him, almost all skin and bone, cloth wrapped around his waist and head, yet with a crazed mop of Don King hair. He sat down next to our Electric Dwarf, and leant over to speak to him conspiratorially with a surprisingly reedy voice. He possessed a heavily-accented yet clear English, and didn't hesitate before explaining,

'I am knowing who you are, Edward. Don't be surprised or scared, please, there is no needing for that. Edward, the thing is going like this, okay? I am thinking that you are a very wealthy individual, amazingly wealthy in fact as individual. . . but not in spirit, more in the area of material riches. I have a message to relay to you, that I am speaking of great monies here. I urge you to do the right thing, as I know that here' – the man touches his head and his heart – 'you have a good soul within. It is just that you are going too far, too far indeed. Don't go too far, Edward, or else you will be beyond our reach, too far away. I fear that my visit to you falls already too late, and that I should have come to be at your side earlier on your journey, but there is no point in regretting this now, we must be moving on. You must open your mind, as I think you have misunderstood the advice of one of your own countrymen, the great W. H. Auden.

Man needs escape, as he needs food and deep sleep.

You have found your escape, at least for now, by coming all this way in a shiny metal tube, known since many years now as the jet aeroplane. Nevertheless, for you to find inner peace and tranquility you will be needing nourishment, fine feedings and deep drinkings, and the sanctuary of sleep. Take my advice, sleep, sleep, then sleep some more. When you awake, you will need to eat . . . and then eat some more. Purify your soul and mind with much water. You need to build up your strength, for you have a great mission ahead of you to fulfil.'

And at this, the semi-naked guru with long grey hair drifted off, finding his vanishing point in no time. Indeed, time itself passed at its own steady rate, and Norman/Edward/Electric Dwarf sat in the same spot on the beach, numb and confused, yet somehow serene. The visit from the kind man had calmed him, relaxed him to a point that he had never known could exist, and he was at one with the world. Ed didn't know who he was anymore, or what day it was, where he was or even what year it was. The main benefit of all of this was that he found himself in a situation where he didn't care. In fact, he'd reached a point in his existence where he didn't care at all. All of these factors – date, location, identity, time – were unknown, deep mysteries, but Ed wasn't even in a state to question these matters, he quite simply existed, and just *was*. If it posed no issue to him, did it matter at all?

And so it came to pass that Ed fell into a deep sleep, the best in weeks, perhaps months. The beach was nearly empty, just a stray dog exploring a fallen tree trunk, and a couple sat in the distance under the curlicue sky. It was pleasantly warm, a rare breeze from the sea drifting inland. Ed's matted beard brushed the warm sand, and he rested his head on some dreaded hair on the side of his head, using it as a cushion. The green flash at sunset had been incredible, especially in Ed's drug-addled brain. Unbelievable smaragdine effects washed over the ocean, astounding the funny little man. It had given him a sense of wonder, and now he let his weariness take over and he slept early, allowing the ocean's music to lull him. He couldn't tell if he was dreaming as everything seemed so real in his state of comatose, yet he saw a cloud drifting across the open beach towards him. It stopped a few metres away.

The ex-England football star Paul Gascoigne was standing in the middle of the cloud, as if swaddled neatly in a giant bubble of cotton wool. He appeared to be cooking some meat on a barbecue. The skin on his gaunt face looked like a leather bag, taut and tanned by the Indian sun perhaps, yet his complexion was clear. It was hard to tell what he was saying, but he was muttering something happily to himself as he concentrated on the task in hand. Suddenly, he gazed over with kind eyes, giving a look which Ed took to mean compassion. He smiled before speaking softly with his kind but fragile voice.

PG: *Hello Edward, it's great to finally meet you. My name is Paul. You haven't been eating properly recently, and I am concerned. I will cook you some Good Meat to restore your energy, and provide you with much-needed fortitude. You need to understand that rather like for a footballer in training, nutrition is important for everyone. You must eat. Forget a light dinner, let's have a heavy dinner together . . . live a little! Rick has left us, I will look after you well so do not fear. I also need to eat in order to regain my strength, we will dine so we can get to know one another while partaking in meat.*

Oh, look! These wonderful sausages are ready. Aren't we lucky?!!

Tell me one thing. May I furnish you with curry sauce on your sausage, Edward?'

THE END

TIM VINE is a renowned musician, known primarily as a pianist and keyboard player. Born in Jersey, his career is extremely varied. Growing up in a musical family, he was a chorister at St. Paul's Cathedral in London from the age of seven. A music scholarship to Cranleigh School followed, then regular lessons and workshops at the Weekend Arts College in Kentish Town, mainly taught by Ian Carr. He later attended Berklee College of Music in Boston, USA, with personal sponsorship from Phil Collins and a scholarship. He has toured and/or recorded with Groove Armada, Noisettes, Moloko, Simply Red, Wilco Johnson, Malcolm McLaren, Terence Trent D'Arby, Paul 'Trouble' Anderson, US3, Incognito, Marlena Shaw, Art Farmer, Baby D, Toploader, Nellee Hooper, Howie Day, The Pasadenas, Jimmy Witherspoon, Pee Wee Ellis, Doc Gyneco and Kid Creole & the Coconuts amoung others. Tim now lives between Paris and London and has written the music for *The Musical of Dorian Gray* as well as appearing in the short film *Jet-Pack Willy.*